I'm in Love with a Thug 3

A novel by Lady Lissa

CHAPTER ONE

Lexus

I was really having a hard time understanding what Taj had told me. He actually said that my brother had paid him to kill my daddy. My brother had wanted our daddy dead. I couldn't believe that Princeton was the one responsible for killing my daddy. I knew that he had been feeling some kind of way about how he claimed my dad was treating him.

I wasn't around them when they were conducting business, so I never witnessed anything. However, I was around them at home and my dad showed all of us nothing but love. How could he have let his feelings get so out of control that he would take it upon himself to take my daddy away from us?

Someone had to be the boss of the business and since it belonged to my dad, of course that role fell on his shoulders. How would it have looked if

Princeton was allowed to run my dad's business while my dad just sat there like a bump on a log?

"How could he do that to our daddy?" I cried as Zay drove us home.

"I don't know, but Taj said he thought your dad and Alize were having an affair. I guess that's where his fury came from," he said.

"Bullshit! He knows how much my dad loved my mom and that my dad would have never cheated on her. My dad was faithful to my mom once they got married. And Alize? Alize loved him, even though he cheated on her and treated her like shit! She would have never cheated on him, especially not with my dad!" I continued to cry.

"Lex, please don't worry about this. I need you to trust me, baby. I need you to trust that I will handle this shit for you. Do you trust me, baby?" he asked as he turned his gaze over to me.

"Of course, I trust you." I said, and I meant it.

"Then let me handle it. You're pregnant with our first child, so please stop stressing yourself out about this. It isn't good for you and it sure ain't good for the baby," he said while stroking my hand that he now held in his.

"I just can't believe Princeton would do something like this. How am I gonna break this news to my mom? She is going to be devastated."

"Babe, do you really think that's a good idea? I mean, your mom has been through so much already. Do you think we should put that on her right now?" he asked.

I turned to look at him as if he had lost his mind. How could he not want me to tell my mom that her only son was responsible for the death of her husband?

"Well, what do you suggest, baby? Because I can't keep this from my mom."

"Just give me a little time to get to the bottom of this before you tell her."

"Bullshit! Taj told us that my brother hired him to kill my dad and I believe him. And my brother had the nerve to tell him that he killed Alize too. His actions have gotten way out of hand. Are we supposed to wait around for him to kill someone else in our family?" I asked.

I needed Zay to take this shit seriously. I knew he was probably downplaying how he really felt because he didn't want to upset me. I knew that I was pregnant, and I needed to stay calm because of the baby, but this was my beloved father we were talking about. My father loved his family more than anything and he was a wonderful provider. I just missed him so much. My brother had to pay for this, even if I would have to be the one that had to deliver the final blow.

But I thought that I'd take Zay's advice and hold off on telling my mom for a little bit. She had been through a lot and my dad had only been gone for four months. This news would surely destroy her; knowing that her son killed the love of her life.

I did notice a change in my brother since the death of my father, but I figured it was his way of dealing with his grief. I never in this lifetime would've thought that his behavior was actually because he was celebrating my dad's death.

"Zay, where are we going?"

"I have a surprise for you. I was gonna wait until your birthday tomorrow, but after everything you've been through today, I think you could use a little pick me up." He smiled at me. He was right about that. I didn't know what his surprise was, but I could definitely use a boost in my spirits.

As much as I loved this man, I didn't have it in me right now to smile, even with him. My heart had been broken by one of the people I thought I could trust most in the world. My brother had committed the ultimate betrayal against our family.

"It's going be alright bae, I promise. If your brother was responsible for killing your dad, he'll get dealt with. I just need you to trust me enough to let me handle it," he said.

I knew when Zay said someone was gonna get dealt with, it meant he was going to kill them. I could have said no; that I didn't want him to kill my brother. But the truth of the matter was that I wanted Princeton dead. I wanted to be there, and I'd even pull the trigger for the pain and agony that he had caused our family. Zay said I wasn't about that life, well maybe it was time that I learned to be about that life.

I was a gangster's daughter and now I was a gangster's lady. Maybe it was time I learned how to fire a gun and be about all that shit. I wasn't a little girl anymore, so from now on, when life threw me a handful of lemons, I'd make lemonade with it.

About 45 minutes later, Zay pulled up to a beautiful brick home. From what I could tell from the streetlights, the lawn was absolutely beautiful. There were a couple of big oak trees in the front yard and beautiful flowers along the front walkway leading into the house. This house was absolutely beautiful.

"What are we doing here? Whose house is this and why are we here in the middle of the night?" I asked as I looked around. I didn't want anyone calling the cops on us, thinking that we were trying to break into their shit. When he used a garage door opener to open up the garage, I almost had a cow.

"Why are you parking in these people's garage? Have you lost your mind, Xavier? Take me home now before these people call the cops on our black asses!" I shrieked.

"Will you calm down? Take these keys and go inside. I'll be there in a minute," he said.

"You're kidding, right?"

"Please bae. You just said you trust me. Was that a lie?" he asked.

"No but…" I started to say.

"No buts, just do what I asked you to do, and I'll be there in a minute," he said before planting a soft kiss on my lips.

Against my better judgment, I opened the passenger's door and slid out the front seat. I used the key he gave me to unlock the door and walked in. As soon as I walked into the kitchen, my mouth hit the floor and tears immediately began to fall.

CHAPTER TWO

Xavier

Lexus was something else. That girl was gonna give me a heart attack. Trying to get her to go inside the house was like a dentist pulling teeth. I was gonna wait until after her birthday party to surprise her with this, but she needed this right now. I opened the glove compartment and pulled out what I needed to make this night even more special for her. I said a silent prayer to the two big men upstairs, God and Big Jim. I needed their approval first and once I felt I had it, I got out of the truck.

I walked into the kitchen to find my baby in tears. What she didn't know before she walked in was that her family was waiting inside for us. I had Ms. Yvonne, Lacey and Ja'Kyra come over. They let themselves in with the extra key I had under the flowerpot on the patio. They filled the kitchen with white balloons and red roses, so that when she walked in, she would see them immediately. She turned to look at me with tears in her eyes and ran into my arms. I lifted her up and held her close to me. She was crying so much that I could feel her tears on my neck.

"When did you do this?" she asked as I put her down.

"Of course, we helped him," said her mom as she turned in shock to see her family; well, her mom and sisters anyway. I didn't want her brother anywhere near us for this special occasion. The only people we needed here were the ones who supported us and our relationship.

"Mommy, what are you guys doing here?" she asked as she went to hug her mom and sisters.

"Zay said y'all had some special news to share with us. He also wanted us to bring all these balloons and flowers for you. You know, you really have a special young man there, honey. You need to hold on to him. He reminds me so much of your father." Ms. Yvonne said with tears in her eyes.

"But wait. Whose house are we in? Where are the people who own it?" Lexus asked us with a confused and perplexed look on her face. "Mommy, don't tell me y'all are finally moving out of the brownstone."

"Uh, not exactly," Ms. Yvonne said.

Whew! I took a deep breath, approached Lexus and got down on one knee. Her hand immediately flew to her open mouth as more tears rolled down her cheeks. Her mom also had tears in her eyes as she watched me propose to her daughter. I was sure she was thinking about her husband and how much she wished he was here to share in this special moment.

"Zay, what are you doing?" Lexus asked as she wiped her eyes with the back of her hand.

"Lex, ever since I first laid eyes on you, I knew you were the woman for me. I felt an instant connection with you the moment I touched your soft skin. That first kiss we shared sent fireworks going off inside me. It was and still is like the fourth of

July every time we kiss. Shiiiddddd, if I get anymore fireworks, my insides gon' be burnt to ashes," I said as everyone laughed. "You came into my life when I wasn't even looking for anyone. I grew up without a family for the past eight years and until I met your family, I had forgotten what it felt like to belong to a family. I feel blessed to be a part of a loving family, it's something I ain't never had. You all are wonderful to me and I just want to be a part of your family forever. I want to be your husband and the father of your children. With that being said, Lexus Belle Clark, will you do me the honors of becoming my wife?" I asked with tears threatening to fall from my eyes again. A nigga had to get it together. That was twice in one day I almost cried like a lil punk.

I opened the small velvet box to reveal a flawless three carat round diamond, encircled with more round diamonds on both sides. The ring was set in 14K white gold and from the expression on her face, I could tell that she loved it. I looked to her mom and sisters, who all had tears in their eyes. She continued to look at the ring as tears kept falling from her already swollen eyes.

"Babe, are you gonna make me the happiest man in the world and marry me or nah?" I asked again.

"YES! YES! Of course, I'll marry you!" she said and jumped into my arms as her family clapped from behind her.

I slid the ring onto her finger, and she grabbed both sides of my face, pulling me in for a kiss. And just as I predicted, the fireworks went off again.

"Ahem," her sister, Ja'Kyra said, causing us to break apart. They surrounded us, offering warm hugs and well wishes. We were all in tears at that point. Yes, even me. As hard as I tried to fight them and keep them from falling, those suckas betrayed me.

"Congratulations to both of you. Zay, I couldn't have asked for a better son-in-law for myself or a better husband for my daughter. Let me be the first to officially welcome you to the family!" Ms. Yvonne said as she embraced me.

"Thank y'all so much for everything," I said.

"I'm going to throw you the biggest wedding this town has ever seen," Ms. Yvonne said.

"Thanks mom," Lexus said.

"Yea thanks, Ms. Yvonne. I'm sure Lexus will appreciate the help to pull everything together. I'll be paying for everything though. Y'all can do it as big as y'all want to, but make no mistake about it, this one is on me," I said as we all started laughing.

"Well, alright then," Ja'Kyra said.

"Mom, there's something else we need to tell you," Lexus said as everybody stood there looking at her.

"Oh God, please don't let it be bad news," Ms. Yvonne prayed. I got a little nervous when Lexus said that. I wasn't sure if she was going to tell her mom about Princeton or what. I hoped that she wouldn't say anything since I promised her that I would handle it.

She looked at me and grabbed my hand. "No, actually it's wonderful news. We're pregnant!"

"What?! You mean my baby is having a baby?! Oh my God!" Her mom screamed and wrapped Lexus in her arms again, a whole new set of fresh tears falling from her eyes.

"I'm gonna be an auntie?" Lacey asked with a huge smile on her face.

"You sure are, squirt!" I said as I gave her a hug.

"Wow! I'm gonna have two babies, Princeton's baby girl and now Lexus'," Lacey beamed.

"When did you find out? How far along are you?" Ms. Yvonne asked.

"Gosh mom, give them a chance to answer," Ja'Kyra said as we burst into laughter.

"We found out earlier today and I'm about eighteen weeks along," Lexus said.

"Wow! And all this time I thought you were just gaining weight and getting fat," Ja'Kyra said as she cracked up.

"Really sis?" Lexus asked as she eyed her sister with a smirk on her face.

"Oh my God! What a wonderful night this has turned out to be, but we gotta get going," Ms. Yvonne said.

"Going? What do you mean, you're leaving? So, this isn't your house? I just figured since y'all were here that maybe this was the house that daddy had been promising to buy you, well us," Lexus said.

"No honey, this house isn't mine," her mom said.

"Then whose house is it?" Lexus asked, facing me with a questionable gaze.

I guess it was time to let the cat out of the bag. I had purchased this house for us to move into after her birthday, but with the night she had, I thought she deserved to feel some sense of security.

"SURPRISE!" I said as I beamed happily.

"Surprise? What do you mean surprise?" Lexus asked.

"This is our house!" I said with a huge smile.

"Shut up! What do you mean our house?" she asked.

"I mean, this is our home! I bought it for us!" I said.

"What?! You bought me a house?" she screamed.

"Us babe, I bought us a house!" I smiled.

"Oh my God! Baby, thank you! Thank you! Thank you!" she said, raining kisses on my face and lips.

"Ewwww!" said Lacey.

"And that is our cue to leave," Ja'Kyra said.

"Yea, we'll talk to you guys tomorrow," Ms. Yvonne said.

"Yea, thank y'all so much for being here and for getting the house together for me," I said.

"There's no place else we would have rather been and we enjoyed every minute of it," Ms. Yvonne said.

"Yea, the only thing missing was a cake and some champagne," Ja'Kyra said. We hugged each other as we said our goodbyes.

Once the family had left and I had my baby all to myself, I scooped her sexy ass up and carried her to our bedroom. I had spent weeks getting this house ready for this day. I slowly put her down and began to remove her clothes while kissing her.

"This room is so beautiful!" she said.

"Not nearly as beautiful as you," I said.

I removed her shirt and kneeled before her, placing my hands on her baby bump. Funny how I never noticed the bump before we went to the doctor. But now that we knew we were having a baby it was very visible. I kissed her belly and rubbed it as she stared down at me stroking my hair.

"I love you so much," I said, looking up at her.

"I love you more," she said.

I pulled down her shorts and panties, immediately placing my mouth on her swollen clit. She moaned as I slowly pushed her back on the bench at the foot of the bed. She told me how she always wanted one, so I knew I had to buy it. She sat down on the bench and opened her legs for me. I used my fingers to part her soft wet folds as I began to eat my snack. Her pussy tasted so sweet, I wanted to stay there all night. But my dick was dying to get in that pregnant pussy, so after munching on her goodies for another five minutes, I pulled my dick out and thrust it inside her. She screamed in pleasure as she bucked on my dick.

I plunged into her as she held onto me and kissed me fervently. I picked her up and held her ass as I slid her pussy up and down on my dick. She cried out in my ear as her body shivered in my arms. I knew she had let her nut go and I smiled, knowing that I was the one responsible for making her feel good. I gently laid her on the bed and got in the missionary position, giving her slow and deep strokes.

She moaned softly at first, but then her cries became louder as she tried to bite down on her lip to keep the noise down. When my boys used to talk to me about how they fucked their pregnant girlfriends, I used to roll my eyes thinking that they were exaggerating. But being inside Lexus' pussy while she was carrying our child was like sitting on cloud nine.

I was definitely in heaven as I lifted her legs higher, so I could get in it deeper. She pulled my face close and gave me a kiss with so much passion, I just knew our souls were about to catch on fire.

I grinded my hips into her, adding just enough pressure until I could feel her creamy satisfaction pouring all over my stick. I loved this woman so much and now that she had agreed to marry me, there was nothing I wouldn't do to keep her happy.

"I want it from the back," she cooed.

"Your wish is my command, baby. Turn yo sexy ass around," I said.

She did as I asked and looking at her pussy from behind made me want to taste it again. I began to lick her dry as I sucked all of her sweet juices. I brought my tongue to her asshole and stuck it in there. She was a little tense at first, but she soon relaxed. I mean, it wasn't like that was my first time licking that spot. She was going crazy with lust as she looked back at me. Damn! That girl knew she was sexy and when she bit down on her lip like that. Shit, I couldn't wait any longer and drove my dick into her full throttle.

She gasped as if she was short winded, but it didn't take long for her to catch her breath again and start throwing that pussy back at me.

"That's right, baby, throw that pussy at ya man!" I said.

She was throwing her pussy and I was throwing my dick. There was so much throwing going on between us, you would've sworn we were at a Mardi Gras parade throwing beads instead of making love. Her body succumbed to the feelings she could no longer hold back. I soon saw the contents of her pussy on my dick, which turned me on even more.

Knowing that I satisfied this beautiful creature made me want to pile drive that pussy to ecstasy. I plunged deeper and deeper, until I could feel the bottom, causing her to scream my name and grip the sheets.

I continued to give her what I knew she wanted until I finally erupted like the geyser in Yellowstone National Park. I sprayed my milk all inside those sugary walls and then we fell on the bed. She put her head on my arm and soon we were knocked the fuck out. Don't laugh niggas because y'all know a woman with some good, pregnant pussy would knock any nigga out.

CHAPTER THREE

Princeton

I had been looking for that muthafuckin' Taj for the past month and that nigga had yet to answer one fucking phone call. When I got my hands on that muthafucka, he would wish he was dead. Lying in bed next to Malaysia had me feeling some kinda way. As I watched her sleep, I looked down at her belly, it was starting to get a little round shape to it. I looked down at her legs and noticed the welts from the belt whooping I had given her ass. They were almost invisible. I touched her stomach and just rubbed it. She was carrying my seed and life was a beautiful thing.

I may not have been the best man for any woman, but one thing I could say about myself was that I was a great father. Zoey didn't have to ask for shit for my little Princess because I always made sure my baby had everything she needed. She just liked to be a bitch about shit. Now that she knew about Malaysia, she didn't want to bring the baby around my crib. That shit was gonna end today.

I wasn't about to take orders from that bitch after I knocked off my old man because I didn't wanna take orders from his ass. What made her any different than my old man? Not a fucking thing! If she wanted some dead man walking, she sure could get it because there was plenty more where that came from.

And if Taj didn't answer his fucking phone, soon there would be two fucking bodies instead of one. Malaysia began to stir in her sleep, backing her ass against my already hard dick. Shiiiddddd! I knew what that meant, and I didn't hesitate to get closer to her. I lifted her leg up and inserted my dick.

I mean, the way she had backed her ass up on me, it was like there was a sign hanging over her pussy that read 'insert dick here', so that was exactly what I did. I grabbed her big milky breasts in each hand as I slammed into her from behind.

She moaned as she lifted her leg higher, allowing me greater access to the pussy that my dick so desperately wanted.

"Who this pussy for?" I asked.

"You baby, only you," she crooned.

"Do you love me, Malaysia?" I asked, even though I already knew the answer.

"Yes Princeton, I love you!" she screamed as I fucked her harder.

I kept giving it to her as she screamed my name and told me how much she loved me and my dick. I wanted to get all up in that pussy as I pumped into her harder. I didn't know if I was in love with Malaysia, but I did know that I cared a lot about this girl. I had to kiss her ass a bunch of times to get her to forget what she saw back at the office with Roz, especially with the missing person's report that kept flashing on the news.

Her family posted missing person fliers all over the place to. They could turn this fucking world upside down, but they would never find that grimy bitch's body. After my boys raped her ass that night, we took her to the crematorium at Freddy's Funeral Parlor and cremated that bitch. She wasn't nothing but ashes now, so they could search all they wanted to. They would never find her, at least not in this lifetime. Good riddance to that messy bitch.

I pumped a few more times into Malaysia's backside and released like a big dog. I laid on my back, taking in deep breaths as I tried to bring my breathing back down to normal. She laid beside me as if she was in deep thought.

Out of the blue, she asked, "What did you do with that chick the other night?"

"What chick?" I asked, as if I didn't know who or what she was talking about. I thought we had agreed to not discuss that shit anymore. I guess I was wrong. I really hated when Malaysia behaved in such a disobedient manner. That always meant I had to come out of pocket on that ass.

"That chick Roz," she said.

"Now, you know damn well I didn't do nothing to nobody named Roz," I said.

I didn't want to hurt Malaysia, but she really needed to mind her own fucking business. All I needed her to do was fuck me, suck me, and shut the fuck up about my business. It made no sense that she constantly wanted to put her nose in my business affairs that didn't have shit to do with her.

"I know she was at the office and now she's missing," she said.

"You know what? It would really be in your best interest for you to forget about what you saw that night," I advised.

She leaned up on her elbow and faced me. "Are you threatening me, Princeton?"

"Baby girl, you should know me well enough by now to know that I'm not one to make idle threats. I make promises and if I promise you something, trust and believe, I will keep that promise." I said.

"Why not just tell her family where she is, so they can have closure?"

I sat up and grabbed her face, squeezing it to make sure she heard me loud and clear. "Do you want to end up like her?" The fear in her eyes, as well as the tears falling down her face let me know that she didn't want to meet the same fate as Roz.

"Do you?" I asked.

She shook her head no.

"Good. I don't want to kill you baby girl, especially since you're carrying my seed. But you really need to mind your own business, yo," I said. "I'm getting tired of telling you to stay out of my shit, yo." I let go of her face and laid on my back. "Now, come and suck my dick to make up for that unruly bullshit behavior."

She wiped her tears and grabbed my dick, taking it in her mouth. She began to suck and slob on my dick; the girl knew how to suck a dick. I held her head and pumped my dick in her mouth. I fucked her mouth until I busted in it. She started gagging and I said, "If you spit out my seeds, I will fuck you up, and I don't mean that in a good way either."

She got teary eyed again as she swallowed my semen down her throat.

"Good girl. Now, go brush your damn teeth. And don't forget to gurgle with that fuckin' mouthwash. I ain't kissing you if your breath smell like cum," I said as she walked to the bathroom.

I climbed out of bed and walked in the bathroom. I turned on the shower and got in. When she finished brushing her teeth, she tried to sneak out of the room, but I called to her. "Get yo ass in here."

She turned around and walked towards the shower. She slid the glass door open and stepped in the shower with me. She began to lather herself with soap and I came up behind her, grabbed her breasts and pumped my hard dick into her. She cried out as she held on to the shower handle.

I fucked her like I was a nigga fresh outta prison after doing three years. I wanted to punish that pussy and leave a mark on it, so she would know who that pussy was for. I grabbed her waist with one hand and pulled her hair with the other, fucking her hard from behind while the water rained down on us. She cried out, practically screaming as I beat that kitty up.

I was so into fucking Malaysia that I almost didn't hear the doorbell ringing. I kept pumping my dick into her pussy, ignoring the chime in an effort to bust this nut. But the ringing of the doorbell persisted, so I pulled my dick out of Malaysia's wet spot, gave her a wet kiss, slapped her ass and stepped out of the shower.

"Don't go anywhere! I'll be right back," I said, blowing her a kiss. She rolled her eyes as she watched me dry myself off and drape a towel around my waist.

I ran to answer the door, so I could get rid of whoever it was. But when I opened the door there was Zoey standing there looking pissed to the max. At least that was how she looked until she saw me standing there, bare chested with nothing but a towel wrapped around my waist. Once she saw me half naked, I could see the lust in her eyes.

"Why the fuck you ringing my fuckin' bell like that? Matter fact, why the fuck are you here, Zoey? And why did you come here without calling first?" I asked, agitation clear in my tone.

"Well, I called you, but you didn't answer your damn phone. But I guess you were in the shower, huh? I remember when we used to take those hot showers together. Do you remember those times?" she said as she licked her lips.

"What the fuck do you want, Zoey? I ain't got time for your bullshit today and I was in the middle of something," I said as she pushed her way into my place.

"I wanted to talk to you about something, but now you got me all horny and whatnot," she said as she reached for my towel.

"Say what you need to say girl and get the fuck out, yo. I told you I was in the middle of something," I said as I pushed her away.

"Now, is that any way to talk to the mother of your only child? You know can't nobody make you feel like I can, zaddy. And looking at you and seeing that look in your eyes, I know you still want me," she said as she stepped closer to me. "We had some amazing sex back in the day. If I know anything, that was the one thing we were good at."

She reached for my towel again and this time I didn't stop her. I allowed her to drop the towel, revealing my hard dick. "Is this what you want?"

She didn't bother to answer. She just dropped down to her knees and began to stroke and suck my dick. I forgot how good she used to rock my mic, but the memories definitely came flooding back once she wrapped her lips around my dick. Once she started sucking my pipe, I began to get into it.

Next thing I knew, I was fucking her mouth as hard as if it was her pussy. I couldn't help it though because that shit felt good as fuck. That girl knew she could suck a dick. Her head game was off the Richter scale. She was sucking my dick so good that I had totally forgotten about Malaysia being in the apartment.

That was until she came running into the room and grabbed Zoey by her hair and began to punch her in the face. She had Zoey in a vulnerable position since she was already on her knees with my dick in her mouth. I saw Malaysia coming, but the head was feeling so good that all I could do was open my eyes.

"You bitch! You come into my house to suck my nigga's dick! I'm about to wipe the floor with yo triflin' ass!" Malaysia yelled as she jumped on top of Zoey and punched her in the face again.

"Bitch, get the fuck off me!" Zoey yelled as she tried to push Malaysia off of her.

I could have stopped them, but this shit was kind of amusing to me. I picked up my towel and wrapped it back around my waist as the two continued to duke it out. After Zoey's lip started to bleed and her right eye was swollen, I pulled Malaysia off of her. Shit, I didn't want the bitch to bleed on my carpet. It always amazed me how stupid some women could be.

I mean, Zoey wasn't raping me; I gave her my dick so she could suck it. Yet, here Malaysia was, beating her like crazy for something that was completely my fault. If I didn't want Zoey to suck my dick, she would have never gotten close enough to my shit to put it in her mouth. But the truth was I wasn't finished fucking Malaysia when Zoey knocked on the door. So, when she offered to slob on the knob, hell yea I let her.

At the end of the day, I was a fucking man and what kind of man would I be if I turned down a free head job? Fucking right I let her suck it and I would have sprayed my shit down her throat too if Malaysia hadn't come up in here acting like Evander Holyfield.

"You bitch!" Zoey yelled as she lunged for Malaysia, who jumped up and kicked her in the stomach since I was holding her back.

"Aaarrrggghhh!" Zoey screamed as she held onto her stomach.

"Let me go, Princeton!" Malaysia said.

"Not until you calm yo lil ass down. You don't need to be fighting this girl when you pregnant with my kid," I said.

"What? Did you just say this bitch is pregnant?" Zoey asked, a look of hurt on her face. She was already in pain from that ass whooping, but the look she gave me just now was from a broken heart. I didn't know why her heart would have been broken because we hadn't been together since before she got pregnant. I mean, of course she allowed me to hit it every once in a while, but we weren't a couple or anything like that.

"Yes, this bitch is pregnant. I'm the BITCH that's pregnant with MY MAN'S baby and I wish he would let me go because I have no problem whooping yo ass again!" Malaysia yelled.

This shit was getting way outta hand. But for some reason, watching two women fight over me was turning me on. I needed to get Zoey the fuck outta here, so I could fuck Malaysia's pregnant pussy some more.

"You know what? I ain't even gon' try to fight you again because if he was really 'YO MAN', then you wouldn't have caught him with his dick in my mouth. You come out here checkin' me when you really should check ya fuckin' man! Open your eyes girl and realize he ain't worth shit. I'm out this bitch!" Zoey said as she chucked the deuces at us.

"I'll come by later to see my baby and talk about whatever it is you wanted to talk about," I told Zoey as I wrapped my arms around Malaysia.

"Whatever," she said.

Once Zoey was gone, Malaysia turned her rage onto me.

"What the fuck was that, Princeton!"

"What was what?"

"All that shit you was saying to me about being your ride or die! I guess that was all some bullshit, huh?" she cried.

"You really are my ride or die chick, baby. I love being with you," he said.

"Then how come I walked up in here, in the place we staying in together, to find you with yo dick in that tramp's mouth? If you cared about me, that shit would have never happened," she said.

"Okay, maybe I was wrong, but she offered to suck my dick. I mean, it was still hard since you hadn't made me cum yet. I just got a lil weak. When she came at me for a head job, I couldn't resist. You know you my baby and Zoey don't mean shit to me no more," I said.

"Fuck that! How can I be your baby when you out here disrespecting me?" she asked. "I can't believe you did this in our place! How disrespectful can you be?"

"Our place?"

"YES, OUR PLACE!"

"That's funny. Do you pay any bills in this muthafucka?" I asked as I rubbed my goatee while waiting for a response.

"Oh, so this ain't our place because I don't pay bills here? Well, if that's how you feel, then why the fuck am I here?"

"You're here because I want you here with me. You're here because you're my ride or die. But you need to learn how to respect your man."

"Me! You are the one who doesn't respect me!" she said.

"I didn't disrespect you? I never asked Zoey to bring her ass over here! I was in the shower getting it in with you when she barged up in here. Look baby, why are we arguing? You're pregnant and you shouldn't be stressing over no bullshit. What we should be doing is making love," I said as I reached for her.

She slapped my hand away angrily. "Don't touch me! Don't you fuckin' touch me!"

"Oh, I see you want to make this hard on me, huh? That's cool. I got some shit to do today anyway. I'm gonna go get dressed, so I can go handle my business at the warehouse," I said.

"Good, then you can drop me off at my mom's house, since this is YOUR place. I don't wanna be here another minute because I don't feel welcome here anymore."

"Baby, you making a big deal out of nothing. I want you to stay here and I expect you to be here when I get back!"

"The hell! I ain't staying up in here while you go fuck yo baby's mama!" she said. There she went, being all defiant and shit.

"Stay here and I'm not gonna tell you again!" I said.

"Yea alright."

I walked off to go get dressed while she stood there in the middle of the living room, smacking her lips and rolling her eyes. I got dressed, splashed some cologne on and prepared to head out. Only when I looked for my keys to my truck, I realized that they weren't there. I ran to the front door and opened it, looking for my truck, only to find that my fuckin' truck was gone.

"I can't believe that bitch took my fuckin' truck!" I fumed.

I jumped on the phone and called Malaysia.

CHAPTER FOUR

Malaysia

Princeton must have thought that I was the stupidest bitch in the world. We were just having sex in the shower and not even ten minutes later, I walked in the front room to find his dick in that hoe Zoey's mouth. I wasn't about to stay there and have him make an ass out of me, so after he went into the bedroom, I grabbed the keys to his precious truck and hauled ass.

When my phone began to ring, I knew it was Princeton calling about his truck. I let it go to voicemail because I didn't want to hear from him right now. My phone continued to ring, so I finally answered it.

"You better bring my fuckin' truck back here, Malaysia!" he yelled.

"Nah, you can come get it from my mom's place," I said.

"Girl, if you don't bring my fuckin' truck back!" he threatened.

Before I had the chance to answer, I got hit from behind. Immediately, I thought somebody wasn't paying attention to where the fuck they were going and had hit me by accident. But then, I looked back and the car was still coming to slam into me again.

"What the fuck!" I screamed.

"What's the matter and you better not had wrecked my shit either!" he yelled.

"Princeton, someone hit me from behind and oh my God! They just hit me again!" I screamed.

"Where are you?" he asked.

"On Linden, not far from the house. Princeton, hurry because they are hitting the truck on purpose. Oh my God!" I cried as I got hit from behind again.

"I'm gonna call Jude to see if he can head your way. I'm coming, baby," he said. I could hear him getting the keys to his Benz.

"Hurry please," I cried as the black Crown Victoria hit me from behind again.

I started blowing the horn, hoping someone would call the cops while I was talking to Princeton. The car began to pull alongside me, so I slammed on the accelerator.

"Princeton, please hurry!" I yelled as the car pulled alongside of me. I turned to see a gun aimed at my window.

"Oh my God! He has a gun! He's gonna shoot me!" I screamed.

Next thing I heard was a loud BOOM!

I tried to keep the truck on the road, but I couldn't do it! I was watching them while trying to keep an eye on the road, which caused me to slam into a ditch. My body lunged forward, and my head struck the steering wheel right before the airbag deployed. My body was in excruciating pain, but I could hear someone jump out the car. I knew that whoever it was must have been coming to see if they had killed me.

"Shoot up the damn truck and kill that nigga! Hurry the fuck up! I hear sirens!"

I hurriedly slid to the floor as bullets tore through the back of the truck. The last thing I heard were sirens before I passed out.

Princeton

When I called Malaysia, I wasn't expecting her to inform me that someone was trying to run her off the fucking road. I could hear her scream and then shots being fired. Then I heard her scream once more before the line went dead. Jude and I arrived on the scene at the same time to find the firefighters using the jaws of life as they tried to get Malaysia out of the truck. I didn't know if she was alive or dead, but I prayed that she was okay. As I pushed my way through the crowd, trying to find who was in charge, I continued to pray that no harm had come to her or my baby.

"Sir, I'm gonna need you to step back please," the officer said.

"That's my girl in that truck. I need to know what happened to her and if she's gonna be alright," I said.

"What's your name, sir?" the officer asked.

"Princeton Clark and that's my girl, Malaysia in that truck," I said.

"Malaysia and Princeton, what kind of names…" he began.

Before he could finish his statement, I asked, "Are you gonna heckle me about my fuckin' name or are you gonna find out how my girl is doing, you fuckin' pig?"

"Listen here, smart ass, if you want information on your girl, then you need to shut the hell up!" the pig said.

"Just give me the information or do I need to call your captain and tell him about your racist ass? With all the shit that has been going down around the world concerning all y'all pig muthafuckas, you really wanna come at me like that! Maybe I should give your captain a call since I have his number on lock. I'm sure he would be very interested to know how you're treating one of their biggest contributors. So, what's it gonna be?" I asked.

"Alright, shit! You people always getting so technical and shit…"

"Just give me the info, muthafucka!" I was getting real aggravated with this pig. If he kept fucking with me, I might have to put his head on the damn chopping block.

"Well, it is to my understanding that she's been drifting in and out of consciousness since they've been trying to get her out of the truck. Once she's out, they'll take her to the hospital. Do you have any information about who would have wanted your girlfriend dead?" the officer asked.

"What are you talking about? I was under the impression that she was in a car accident," I lied. Of course, I knew that Malaysia's wreck was intentional, but I wasn't about to share that with this pig.

"Oh no! This shit here was no accident. No, somebody shot at your girl's truck and rammed her off the road. So, do you have any idea who could have done this?" he asked again.

"No, I don't, but I need to know if she's alright. She's pregnant!" I yelled.

"Did you say she's pregnant?" the pig asked.

"Yes! Now can you find out how she is?" I asked. I knew the only way I was gonna get this pig to see me as anything more than a thug was to spread sugar all over my words.

He jumped on his radio that was connected to a strap on his shoulder and said, "Hey, the female in the truck is pregnant, so be very careful."

"How far along is she?" someone on the radio asked.

"How far is she?" the pig asked.

"Four and a half months," I said.

"She's four months," he said back into the radio.

After a couple of minutes passed, without any word on Malaysia's condition I asked, "Can you ask how she is? I just want to know if she's still alive."

"The husband is here and wants to know if she's alive," he said.

"She's unconscious, but alive," the paramedic said.

They pulled her slowly out of the truck and placed her on a stretcher. She was unconscious, and she had blood dripping from her left shoulder. I also saw blood on her forehead and yelled, "Malaysia I'm here, baby girl!" I wasn't sure if she could hear me, but I wanted her to know that I was here for her. "Where are they taking her?"

"Where are you taking the girl?" he asked into his radio.

"Brookdale University," was the response of the emergency medical tech that came over the radio.

"Jude, I need you to go over to Malaysia's mom's crib and scoop her up. I'll call her and explain what happened to Malaysia, so she'll be ready when you get there. Bring her to meet me at the hospital," I said.

"You got it, boss," he said and jumped in his ride. I jumped in my Benz and followed the ambulance. I picked up my phone and called Malaysia's mom.

"Hello," she answered.

"Hello, Louise, I don't want you to panic, but Malaysia was in an accident," I said.

"What! She was in an accident? What happened?" she asked.

"I don't know all the specifics, but I'm sending my boy Jude to pick you up and bring you to the hospital. He should be there in about 20 minutes. Please be ready when he gets there," I said.

"Oh my God! My baby was in an accident! Where is she?" she asked, and she sounded like she was crying.

"They're taking her to Brookdale University, I'm headed that way also. Hopefully, by the time you arrive, they'll be able to inform us on her condition. But can you please be ready when Jude gets there?" I asked.

"Who the hell is Jude?"

"He works for me, Louise. Can you please just be ready? He'll pick you up and bring you to the hospital," I explained.

"Fine, I'll be ready," she said.

I ended the call as I pulled into the parking lot of the hospital. I found a parking spot and rushed into the emergency wing of the hospital. I saw the emergency staff rushing Malaysia to the emergency room and I was trying to go with them. I was stopped by a security guard, who directed me to the window for me to talk to a nurse.

"My girlfriend Malaysia was just brought in. Can someone please tell me how she's doing?" I asked.

"How long ago was she brought in?" the woman at the desk asked.

"She was just wheeled back there."

"If she was just wheeled back there, you need to give them a few minutes to assess her injuries. Someone will be with you shortly though. In the meantime, you can fill out this paperwork," she said and handed me a stack of papers connected to a clipboard.

I sighed and went to sit down so I could fill out the paperwork for Malaysia to get the proper treatment. They wanted insurance information. That was easy since I was her insurance. No matter how much her stay here was, I was gonna be responsible.

"Where's my baby?" I heard Louise asking the lady at the window.

I stood up to go talk to her and Jude.

"Louise," I said.

She ran to me and asked, "Where's my baby? How's she doing?"

"She's in the back, but I don't know how she is yet. They said someone would come and speak to us soon," I explained to her the same thing the woman behind the window told me.

"I need to know how she is and I need to know now!" she said as she approached the woman again.

"I need to speak to someone who can tell me what my daughter's condition is!" Louise stated.

"Ma'am, I'll tell you the same thing I told her husband, someone will be out here to speak with you soon," the woman said.

"He is not her husband and lil girl, you got exactly two seconds to get your ass up and go find me a doctor or all hell will break loose in this motherfucking hospital. So, if I were you, I would run my ass back there and don't come back without a doctor who can tell me how my daughter is doing. NOW MOVE YOUR ASS!" she yelled. The woman quickly slid off her seat and flew towards the back to find someone to come speak to Louise.

I had never seen Malaysia's mom act that way before, but like a lioness, when it came to a mother and her cub, she would do anything to protect hers. The young woman returned and pointed in our direction as she spoke to a doctor. The doctor quickly made her way to where we stood. I guess the look on Louise's face told her she better hurry the hell up.

"Are you here for information on Malaysia Hughes?" she asked.

"Yes, she's my daughter and I want to know how she is. Please tell me my baby is going to be okay," Louise said.

"My name is Dr. Kennedy and your daughter was brought in with two gunshot wounds; one to her left shoulder and the other to her left forearm. She also has a laceration to her forehead, which is going to require stitches. We're working to remove the bullets now and stitch up her wounds. Her injuries aren't life threatening, so she should make a full recovery. She may need physical therapy for her arm and shoulder, but otherwise she should be fine," Dr. Kennedy said.

"What about the baby?" I asked.

"The baby is fine. I don't know how she managed to pull it off, but her baby is going to be fine," the doctor said with a smile.

"Thank you so much, Dr. Kennedy. Can you please let us know when she comes out of surgery?" Louise asked.

"Yes ma'am, I will. Now, if you will excuse me, I need to get back in there, so I can tend to your daughter," she said.

Once the doctor was gone, Louise turned on me.

"How could you let this happen? How did my baby just so happen to be in your truck and get shot the fuck up?" she asked.

"She was on her way to see you. I don't know why she got shot!" I said.

"She was driving your truck and got shot! That ain't no damn coincidence!" she said.

"What exactly are you accusing me of?" I asked getting defensive. I didn't know someone was gonna shoot at my damn truck. How the fuck was I supposed to know that?

"I think maybe they meant to shoot you! Everybody loves Malaysia. No one hated my daughter and certainly not enough to want to kill her. But you, you on the other hand, I suspect with all the shit you've done, you have made some enemies since you took over for your dad. I trusted you to protect my daughter and this is where she ends up; in the fuckin' hospital!" she yelled.

"Louise, I mean you no disrespect, but you ain't got to come out of pocket with me like that. I ain't the enemy. I would have never wanted anything to happen to Malaysia, especially when she's pregnant with my child," I said.

"You did this! I don't care what you say. YOU ARE RESPONSIBLE FOR MY BABY

LYING ON THAT OPERATING TABLE! When she's released, she's coming home with me and you're never going to see her again," Louise threatened.

"With all due respect Louise, Malaysia is a grown ass woman and she doesn't need you telling her what to do. She can make her own decisions about where she wants to go when she's released," I said.

"Boooooooyyyyy, I guess you didn't hear me. If I said she's coming home with me, you best believe she's coming home with me. I trusted you to take care of her and you almost got her killed. I've known you ever since we moved here, so I know what you do for a living. I just figured you would keep my daughter safe, especially since she's carrying your baby. But you are bad news and if it's the last thing I do, I will protect my daughter from you!" she said with rage in her eyes.

"I didn't have anything to do with Malaysia getting hit, yo!" I said.

"Just stop lying, Princeton! If you can't be honest with me, don't say shit to me!" she said.

She sat down in one of the chairs and I sat in the opposite corner, attempting to finish filling out the papers. When I was finished, I walked over to the window and handed them to the woman at the desk. I went back to sit down in the chair to wait for the doctor to come back in and give us word on Malaysia's condition. Jude was sitting with me, but he was so quiet, you barely knew he was here.

"Aye man, do you think they were trying to kill you?" Jude finally asked.

"Not here, man," I said.

"Aight," he said.

We sat and waited for the doctor while Louise kept giving me the evil eyes. I guess it was a good thing for me that looks couldn't kill because I would definitely be needing some medical attention or a medical examiner. Finally, after a two hour wait, Dr. Kennedy entered the waiting room with news about Malaysia. We all hurried over to her, so we could hear what she had to say.

"How is she, doctor?" Louise asked.

"She is out of surgery. We were able to remove both bullets and patch her up. We also stitched up the cut on her forehead, which should heal nicely. She's in recovery and the anesthetics are still in effect, so she'll be out for at least a couple of hours. But the good news is that she's stabilized. We'll let you know when she has been moved to a private room so you can see her," the doctor said.

"Thank you, Dr. Kennedy," Louise said.

"Mr. Clark, I'm aware that you will be paying for Malaysia's bill," the doctor said.

"Yes, I will," I said.

"They should be calling for you in the billing department to make sure all your information is correct," she said.

"That's fine. I'll be here," I said.

"Okay well, I will let you know when you can see her," Dr. Kennedy said and retreated back behind those double doors.

I thought about calling Lexus to let her know what happened to Malaysia but decided not to. I didn't want or need any more drama than there already was. The drama between me and Malaysia's mom was enough.

"You're paying for Malaysia's bill?" Louise asked.

"Yea, she's the mother of my child, so why wouldn't I pay?" I asked.

"Since you're the one responsible, why wouldn't you pay? So, if you're expecting me to say thank you, you can forget it. Had it not been for you, this would have never happened," she said. This bitch was so ungrateful. Malaysia and I weren't married, so if I wouldn't pay the bill, she would be stuck with it. She should definitely be thanking me, but she wanted to be stubborn.

"Well damn Louise, you're welcome," I said sarcastically.

She rolled her eyes at me as she went back to her seat. I was about to sit back down in the chair when someone called my name.

"Mr. Princeton Clark," a female called from the doorway.

I stood up and went to where she stood. She told me to follow her, which I did. I followed her to the desk and sat across from her.

"Good afternoon, Mr. Clark. My name is Verna and I'm going to go over the information to make sure it's accurate for our billing department. So, here we go," she said.

I wasn't even sure why she had any questions for me. I mean, it wasn't like the paperwork was years or months old. I had just completed it.

"Are you and Miss Hughes married?" she asked.

"Nah, she's my girl," I said.

"And your phone number is correct also?"

"Ma'am, everything on that paper is correct. I mean, gotdamn, I just filled the shit out a couple hours ago. If y'all worried about not getting paid, put that out your head right now because I can pay you right now. Is that what you need me to do?" I asked.

"No sir, that isn't necessary. But I have to ask these questions, or I wouldn't be doing my job. You don't need to pay the bill just yet. You will get a bill in the mail in a few weeks and you can pay it then. It will be expensive because of the extensive treatment she's receiving. She'll be here for a while, so the office will allow you to make monthly payments until the bill is paid in full," she said.

"Look ma, do I look like a nigga that would be interested in your little payment plans? I mean, my watch probably cost more than your whole damn wardrobe. Shit, soon as the bill comes in, it'll get paid in full that day. So, keep your payment arrangements for some poor sucka that needs it," I said.

She thought I didn't see her roll her big eyes at me behind those fucking Coke bottle glasses, but I saw that bitch. Fuck her and what she thought. Talking about a damn payment plan. I didn't need no fucking payment plan. She would see that shit.

CHAPTER FIVE

Lexus

It had been over a month since I moved in with Zay and I couldn't be happier. The birthday party that he had spent so much money on was a bust because I didn't really feel like celebrating. With the information I had found out about my brother, I was not in a celebratory mood. Zay had been trying his best to cheer me up all week, but even our engagement couldn't perk me up that much. I really wanted my brother dead at this point. I couldn't believe he was responsible for killing my daddy. And to top it off, I heard about Malaysia getting in an accident and being hospitalized.

The news reports were very vague, but they did say Princeton's truck was found in a ditch. Even though they didn't say anything about a shooting, I saw the truck and it was riddled with bullets. I wondered how she was doing and if my brother had anything to do with that "so called" accident.

"Are you okay?" Zay asked, wrapping his arms around my waist and rubbing my swollen belly. At five and a half months, my belly was starting to look like I had swallowed a watermelon, but I loved the feeling. I loved feeling our baby kick when Zay put his hand on my stomach or when he spoke to my belly. We didn't want to know what the sex of our baby was before, but now we wanted to know so we could decorate the nursery appropriately. I couldn't wait to find out.

"I was just thinking about Malaysia. I feel like I should go see her, ya know?" I said as I leaned into him.

"You do know that she got shot, right?" he asked.

"What! I knew she was injured, but I didn't know she had gotten shot!"

"Yea, she was hit twice from what I was told. They rammed the truck off the road and rained bullets through and through," he explained.

"What?! The news didn't say anything like that!" I said. I mean, I knew that his truck had been shot at, but I didn't know that she was shot. The news always left out the most important shit, but I guess they had to do what they had to do to find whoever did the deed.

"I don't think they released that information to the news stations. The police are working on the case I guess and if they leak out too much to the media, they may alert the people they are looking for," he explained.

"I wonder who would do that to her? Who hated her enough to want her dead?" I asked.

"That's just it; I don't think she was the target."

I turned in his arms to face him. "Do you think they were after my brother?"

"Think about it. She was in his truck and the tint on that truck is so dark, you can't see who's in it. I think they were after Princeton, and she just got caught in the middle," he said.

My brother had made some enemies since my dad got killed. As much as I loved him, I wanted him dead too. With that being said, I could only imagine how many others felt the exact same way I did. My brother had made so many careless decisions since he took over my dad's business, so I was sure if someone tried to kill him, that wouldn't be the last attempt on his life.

"What are we going to do about getting him for what he did to my dad? I swear, I just need a handgun and five minutes with that fool," I said.

"And I told you that you ain't about that life. Let me and my niggas handle Princeton," Zay said.

"At least, let me be in on it. I want to be there when you question him or whatever it is you plan on doing with him. I want to know why he did what he did. It couldn't have been just about taking over dad's business."

"Well you remember what Taj said about your dad screwing his girl. I can't believe that nigga even had that in his head."

"He knew that my dad would never cheat on my mom. He just used that as an excuse to get rid of him. I love my brother, but for what he did to my dad and the pain he's caused our family, I can't ever forgive him. Zay, you have to make him pay for that shit or I will. You keep saying I ain't about that life, well, he would be the perfect specimen for me to prove you wrong," I said.

"Damn, you're sexy when you're angry," he said and kissed me.

"Don't start nothing you ain't got time to finish," I said with a smile.

"Oh, trust me, baby, I always have time to finish anything I start with you," he said as he lowered his head and planted his lips to mine again. This time our kiss had more passion and definitely more heat.

He dropped my straps from my nightie off my shoulders and let his lips travel to my neck as I felt the soft satin material around my feet. I wasn't wearing any panties because my hormones were in overdrive and I was always horny. Zay grabbed a swollen breast in each hand and began to lick on my protruding nipples.

I grabbed his head and rubbed it as he continued to lick and suck my breasts. Since my pregnancy, my breasts went from a perfect size C to a blossoming DD size in only a couple of months and my baby was enjoying them immensely.

He slowly pushed me back on the bed and kissed my swollen stomach as his kisses traveled to my inner thighs. He parted my legs and looked at my pussy as if it were a full course meal. He smiled at me as I watched him prepare to dive in.

He licked slowly, causing me to gasp for air. He inserted two fingers inside my wetness and pushed in and out, in and out as I gyrated my hips. He made circular motions with his tongue around my clit, which always drove me crazy.

He licked, sucked, and finger fucked me until I felt myself release. He pulled out his fingers and while looking into my eyes, he licked them clean.

"Mmmmmmm! Your pussy juices are so sweet, tastes like honey," he said as he stood up and dropped his pajama bottoms, revealing just how much he wanted me.

I sat up and took his big dick in my hands, stroking it slowly while kissing his stomach. I licked his mushroom shaped head, teasing it ever so softly with my tongue. I licked up and down his shaft and slowly wrapped my lips around it. I sucked it like it was a Tootsie Roll pop, applying pressure to certain points as he played with my nipples.

When his knees began to quiver, he pulled his dick out of my mouth and gently pushed me back on the bed, leaving my ass hanging at the edge. He bent his knees a little and inserted his dick inside me as he placed both my legs on his shoulders. He squeezed my breasts as his dick went in and out of me. He had me feeling so good right now; I moaned loudly.

I came so many times that I lost count. I didn't know how much longer I would be able to have sex with Zay while I was pregnant, so I was gonna enjoy it while it lasted. I was five and a half months now, so my belly was shaping out into a nice little watermelon.

"Turn over for me baby," he said.

He thrusts two more times before he pulled out and kissed me. I turned over for him to get it from behind. He pushed his dick inside me and smacked my ass as I buried my face in a pillow to keep from screaming too loud. His dick went in and out as my breasts bounced up and down. I threw my ass back at him as he penetrated my pussy with his big dick.

"Oh God! That feels so good!" I cried.

"You love that dick, huh?" he asked breathlessly.

"Oh yaaasssss!" I said.

He pumped into me for several more minutes until we both collapsed next to each other, our sweaty bodies pressed up against each other. We were lying in each other's arms until his phone began to ring.

"Don't answer it," I said.

"I got to, bae. I'm waiting for information about who shot up your brother's whip and confirmation about Princeton ordering the hit on your dad," he said as he reached for his phone.

"Waddup," he answered.

I could hear a voice on the other end that sounded panicked. Zay sprung from the bed and started throwing his clothes on. From his tone, I could tell that he was really upset. I jumped up and grabbed my robe, put it on and tied it at the waist. He started throwing his shoes on and strapped up.

"I'm on my way," he said before he hung up.

"What was that about?" I asked, worried about my man.

"Babe, I'll call you later. I gotta go," he said as he kissed me on the lips.

He grabbed the keys to his black Chevy Silverado and headed for the door. I hurried after him because I needed to know what was going on.

"What's going on?" I asked again.

"Babe, I don't have time to explain now. I'll call you later. I love you," he said.

"I love you too. Babe, please be careful," I said as he slammed the door to the garage.

As I stood in the doorway, he burned rubber out of the garage and down the driveway. All I could do was say a prayer for him to return home safely. I didn't know what was going on with him, but in his line of work, I couldn't help but to worry about him.

CHAPTER SIX

Zay

When the call came in, I'd just finished making love to Lexus. This was the last thing I wanted to deal with. I mean, we were still basking in the afterglow of our love. Then Chico called and said that some Nigerians were at the spot with guns wanting answers about who shot their boss and compadres.

I couldn't believe that they were at our spot after all this time had passed. We expected them to retaliate a lot sooner, but when days, then weeks, then months went by and nothing happened, we just assumed that was the end of it.

Chico said they were threatening to shoot up my place and all my men if I didn't get my ass down there. I flew down 278 at 85 MPH, not wasting any time to get there. I was going as fast as I could. I expected to get stopped by the police at any moment, but thankfully I made it there without incident.

I pulled into the parking lot where there were two huge Nigerians standing guard at the doorway. I jumped out and rushed into the building to find more Nigerians armed with huge guns and my own team, who were pointing their own weapons at them.

"What the fuck is going on here?" I ask.

"Are you de leader of dis bullshit operation?" asked a Nigerian.

"Who the fuck are you?" I asked. I mean, did that muthafucka think I was gon' just come up in here and we was gon' have a kumbaya moment. Hell naw! These niggas was on my territory and my property.

"My name is Tombay. I understand dat you were present when my men were gunned down in an effort to do business with you," he said.

"Okay, first of all, you don't barge into my place of business the way that you did. That's some disrespectful shit! Second, I was scheduled to do business with Taurus and we were just as surprised as you are that they were killed here. I had no idea that someone was waiting to take them down," I said.

"What kind of bullshit operation are you running if you don't know your men?" Tombay asked.

"That's the second time you called my business a bullshit operation. I know that you're upset, but I'm not gonna take too much more of your disrespect. Now, the man who put the wheels in motion for that incident was working for me. He turned out to be a traitor, so his ass is no longer with us," I said.

"So, if not you, then who ordered the hit on my people?" he asked.

"There were a few people that weren't happy with Big Jim doing business with the

Nigerians. I have a feeling that is why he lost his life," I said.

Even though I knew Princeton was behind the ambush that day, there was no way I was going to be a snitch. I lived by the code and if it was meant to be today, I planned to die by the code too.

"Who are dese people you speak of?" he asked.

"I'm not a snitch! If you spend enough time in Brooklyn, you will be able to find out that information for yourself. But I ain't no snitch," I said.

"Then you and your men will die!" he said as they raised their guns at me and my crew.

All of a sudden, the door burst open and about 15 of my men walked in, along with his two guards that were outside. The two guards that were outside now had their hands up and had been disarmed by my crew. I smiled, looked at Tombay and said, "It looks like you are outnumbered, my friend. So, I will make a deal with you. I will spare your life if you get the hell out of here and stay out of my face."

He looked at his men and said, "Stand down." He turned his attention back to me. "It seems you have the upper hand, but make no mistake about it, we will meet again. And when we do, you need to be prepared."

He gave me this menacing look that let me know the shit wasn't over.

"Oh, trust me, I'm always prepared. Just so you know, if it's a war you want, a war is what you will get," I said with a smile.

He made a circular motion over his head with his finger and he and his crew left the building. I looked at my crew and they were still standing in an armed position, like they were ready to light those niggas up like fireworks on the New Year's Eve. Several of them had accompanied our unwelcomed guests outside, just in case they decided to pull something. Once the coast was clear, they returned inside the building to join the rest of us.

"What the fuck was that shit about?" I asked, even though I already knew the answer.

"They wanted to know who killed their boss, but I wasn't about that snitching shit, so I called you. I knew you weren't gonna snitch either, but I knew you would hit up our reinforcement team and whew! Them niggas came just in time too," Chance said as he laughed.

"Those niggas meant business and they're gonna come for us again until they find the information they want. FUCK!!" I said as I banged my fist against the desk.

"What you trippin' on, boss? You ain't the one responsible for that shit," John said.

"Nawl, I ain't, but since we didn't snitch and tell him who did it, them fools gonna hold us accountable. I need to turn up the heat on Princeton's ass, but I don't know how to do it without acting like a bitch ass rat!" I said.

I wasn't no punk by any means, but I'd be damned if I turned into a fucking snitch. If I had to die not to break the fucking code, so be it.

"Y'all know that nigga's girl in the hospital, right?" Chico asked.

"Yea, I think those bullets was meant for his ass. I wonder who put the hit out on him though," Chance said.

"That's the same thing I was thinking. Man, that mu'fugga done made mad enemies, yo. He better watch his back, especially while these Nigerians are in town," I said.

"Fuck that nigga! I want his ass dead my damn self after what he did to Big Jim. That nigga just showed me that he has no loyalty. Hell, if he can kill his own father, what's to stop him from putting a hit out on us? Fuck that nigga!" Chance said.

"In due time, my nigga, he gon' get his in due time. I have plans for Mr. Princeton; for all the shit he been putting my girl and her family through," I said.

"Yea, well on another matter, my fam wanna know when you ready to get that shipment?" Chico asked.

"Whenever they ready, yo. Just let me know," I said.

"Well lemme call this nigga now because this mu'fugga gotta eat. Ya feel me?" Chico asked.

"Yea get with it," I said.

While Chico was on the phone making arrangements for our shipment, I sent the rest of my crew to handle their blocks. I had a couple of dudes that were ride or die material, so I had bumped them up to be my head block lieutenants. That meant that they had lil niggas under them that reported to them while they reported to me. Angel had proved to be one of the realest niggas in my crew, so of course he was a lieutenant. Angel was Chico's cousin and just like his older cousin, Angel was quick to pull the trigger.

"Boss, can I holla at you for a minute?" Angel asked.

"Yea sure," I said as we walked to my office.

I closed the door and said, "Waddup?"

"I just would like for you to trust me, to let me handle that nigga Princeton for you," Angel said.

"Angel, I appreciate the offer and the fact that you have taken the initiative to speak with me about this. Just know that he will get handled. I have to proceed with caution on this one because that nigga is my girl's brother. I can't just kill him without thinkin' about the repercussions from his family, my soon to be family. Ya feel me?" I asked.

"Yea, I gotcha, boss," he said.

"Just keep doing what you do, Angel. I will let you know if I need some help with this one," I said.

"Aight," he said as he dapped me up and we headed out the door.

"Yo, we on for tomorrow night, same time, same place," Chico said.

"Cool," I said.

"Angel, I want you to ride with us tomorrow night. Meet us here at midnight," I said.

"You got it boss," he said.

"I'm gon' hit y'all up later. I'm gonna go home and check on my girl," I said.

"Cool, check you later," Chico said before I left.

I hit up Lexus to let her know I'd be home soon. She wanted to know what went down that caused me to rush out the house earlier. I promised to tell her once I got home. I knew she was worried and that wasn't good for the baby. We had a doctor's appointment tomorrow and we would find out the sex of the baby. I wanted a girl because I knew that she would be just as beautiful as her mom.

But she wanted a baby boy that looked like me. It really didn't matter if we had a boy or girl. As long as our little one was born healthy, that was all that mattered. I would have loved to marry Lexus before we had the baby to make everything legal and shit. But I knew she wanted a big wedding with bridesmaids, flowers, and all that shit. As much as I loved her, I wasn't going to deny her anything that she wanted. After all she had been through, she deserved everything and anything she wanted.

CHAPTER SEVEN

Malaysia

I had been in the hospital for two days when Anthony finally came to see me. I really wasn't expecting to see him, especially since Princeton had been standing guard the whole time. Princeton had finally gone to check on his business and not long after he left, the door opened. I thought it was my mom since she left a little while ago to go get something to eat.

"Hey boo," Anthony said. I sat up in bed, a little nervous because I really didn't know how long Princeton would be gone.

"What are you doing here, Anthony?" I asked.

"I heard you got shot. I came to visit the first night, but your little guard dog didn't leave the damn hospital until today. How are you feeling?" he asked as he held my hand.

"I'm a little better than when I first came in. I'm just in a lot of pain and my body is sore. I appreciate you coming to see me, but you really shouldn't be here," I said.

"Are you kidding? I had to come so I could check on you and the baby," he said as he placed a hand on my stomach, which had gotten pretty round at five months.

"Who told you?" I asked.

I knew I should have told him, but I had already told Princeton, who seemed really happy that I was pregnant. He was also happy to find out that he was going to be a father again. Since he found out about the baby, he hasn't hit me once. He would kill me if he knew this baby was really Anthony's.

"My question for you is why didn't you tell me? You know how much I love you and I would have been here for you. Why didn't you want me to know that I was going to be a father?" he asked.

"Because the baby isn't yours," I lied, hoping that he wouldn't be able to see the truth in my eyes.

"What?! You're lying. I know that's my baby. Why are you lying to me about it? Are you trying to pass my baby off as his?" he asked with a hurt expression on his face.

"That's not even the case. I'm telling you this because it's the truth. This is Princeton's baby."

"Naw, see I know this baby is mine."

"How do you know that?" I asked nervously.

"You just told me."

"What do you mean?" I asked.

"If it really wasn't my baby, you would have just told me that. But instead, you asked how do I know; tell the truth, Malaysia. This is my baby and I know it because I can feel it right here," he said as he touched his chest where his heart was beating. I almost burst out with the truth, but I held my tongue. "I love you so much. Has that nigga ever told you that he loved you?"

Why was he asking me that? How could he say for sure that Princeton had never told me that he loved me? He wasn't always with me and he wasn't a fly on my wall.

"This isn't your baby, Anthony," I said, hoping that he would believe me, even though my voice was trembling.

"It is my baby and you can't lie to me," he said as he rubbed my belly.

My lip started trembling and tears formed in my eyes. I wasn't going to cry; there was no reason to cry. I tried to push his hand away, but he wouldn't move. Call me crazy, but it just felt right to have him touching my stomach. When I thought about the differences between how Anthony treated me and how Princeton treated me, it was clear who really cared about me.

My phone beeped, signaling a text message and jolting me out of my reverie. I snatched my phone off the bedside table, trying not to hurt my shoulder in the process. I could still see the love in Anthony's eyes as he continued to rub my swollen belly.

I wondered if my baby knew it was his or her daddy rubbing my belly because our baby was kicking up a storm as he spoke to my stomach. I unlocked my phone and opened the text message from Princeton.

Princeton: I'm omw…do you need me to get u sumthin?

Me: Wya

Princeton: Passing up the DQ around the corner

Me: Can u get me a medium Oreo blizzard please?

Princeton: Aight

Me: Thnx

Princeton: Yw…c u soon

Me: K

"Anthony, you have to leave. Princeton is on his way," I said.

"Maybe I should wait until he gets here. Maybe it's time for you to tell him the truth. Tell him that this baby is mine and not his!" he said with tears in his eyes.

"I can't do that. You have to go," I repeated.

"Why Malaysia? Why would you tell him my baby is his and not tell me? What does he have that I don't? Is it his money or the power? He doesn't love you like I do. Did you hear me? I love you Malaysia and I want us to be a family. That nigga doesn't give a shit about you."

This was the first time Anthony had said that he loved me since we began sleeping together. I knew he said it before, but for him to say it again. I had a feeling that he had some kind of feelings for me, but to know that he actually loved me kind of put things in perspective for me.

Could I continue this lie and let Princeton believe this was his baby, knowing that it was Anthony's? I had to continue this charade, at least until I came up with a better plan. If Princeton even thought that I had been lying to him, I was as good as dead.

"Do you remember the last time y'all had a face off? You have to go. Please," I begged as I wiped away my own tears.

"Fine, but I'll be back. I love you and I love our baby and I'm not giving up on us," he said as he leaned down and kissed me slow and sensually.

He pulled away from me and made his way out the door. He wasn't gone but five minutes when Princeton walked in with my blizzard from Dairy Queen. He handed me the cup and sat in the chair next to my bed, grabbed the remote control, and began flipping through the channels until he found the basketball game he was looking for.

"Thanks for the blizzard and I'm fine, thank you for asking," I said, my voice dripping with sarcasm.

He didn't even bother to respond as he watched the game on the flat screen television. I ate my blizzard, although I wasn't really hungry for it. The only reason I asked for it in the first place was because Anthony was here. I didn't want Princeton to show up while he was here, so I had to find a way to stall him. I didn't need another confrontation between them, especially while I was laid up this hospital room recovering from gunshot wounds. When I was first told that I had gotten shot, I couldn't believe it. Who would shoot me?

As I replayed that incident over and over in my head, I still couldn't understand why anyone would hate me enough to want me dead. I wondered if Zay knew what happened to me. It had been two days and he hadn't come by or called, so maybe he didn't even know. I should probably shoot him a text message in case he didn't know. I knew that he would be worried about me and come to check on me, send me flowers or something. Before I got around to sending that text, my mom walked in with two detectives.

"Hey baby, how are you feeling?" she asked.

"I'm okay, mom," I said as she gave me a kiss on the cheek.

"I met up with these two detectives in the hallway. They want to ask you some questions about what happened to you that day," she said.

"Well hello, Mr. Clark, right?" the detective asked Princeton.

Princeton looked at him and sneered, "Detective."

"It's fancy meeting you here again," the detective said with a sneer of his own.

"So, you know him?" my mom asked.

The first thing that crossed my mind was, *this cannot be good.* My mom already thought I was in here because someone was aiming for Princeton that day. Before she had so much respect for him, now she couldn't stand him.

"Oh yes, we brought Mr. Clark in for questioning when the body of his former girlfriend turned up. She was murdered and since he was the last person to see her alive, he had to be questioned," the detective said.

"Man, can you just get to the reason why you here? I'm sure you didn't come here just to talk about me," Princeton said with an attitude.

"No, we actually came here to question Miss Hughes; seeing you here was just a bonus," he smiled at Princeton.

"Whatever! Can you just get to the damn reason why you here?" Princeton snarled.

I couldn't understand what he was angry about. I mean, I was the one who got shot. I was the one lying in a hospital bed with stitches in my arm, shoulder and forehead. I was the one who almost got killed that day. So, why the hell was he so angry?

CHAPTER EIGHT

Princeton

Malaysia thought her ass was slick, but I knew what time it was. I saw that nigga coming out of that room just as plain as I could see the nose on my fucking face. Then when I got to the room, she wanted to catch an attitude because I didn't ask how she was doing. Well apparently, she was doing just fine since her nigga came to see her today.

I had every intention of letting her in on my little information, which happened to be her lil secret, but I decided to keep that little tidbit of information to myself. I would let her know what I know real soon though. I wasn't the one to hold my tongue for foolishness.

When her mom came in with those fucking detectives that questioned me about Alize's murder, I was ready to head for the hills. But, had I done that, they would have thought that was a suspicious move. I didn't need to give those muthafuckas any more leverage.

"What can I do for you detectives?" Malaysia asked.

"We need to know what happened to you on the day you got shot. Do you remember anything that happened that day?" Detective Ashford asked.

"I remember riding down the street and getting hit from behind. When I looked in the rearview mirror, I saw a black Crown Victoria with dark tint on the windows. The driver of the car hit me three more times before they pulled alongside me and opened fire," she said.

That was the same car that tried to get at me that day, but I wasn't about to tell that to these bullshit detectives. They were just looking to put a nigga behind bars anyway.

"So, they struck you from behind how many times?" Detective Ashford asked.

"Four times," she said.

"And then they pulled beside you and opened fire, is that correct?" Detective Palmer asked.

"Yes," she said.

"Were you able to get a look at the shooter?" Detective Ashford asked.

"No, I was too busy trying to keep the truck on the road while trying to stay alive! All I saw was the barrel of a gun," she said.

"And then what happened?"

"I lost control of the truck and hit the ditch. That's when I heard someone say to shoot up the truck and kill that nigga," she said.

"Is there anyone you know of who would want to hurt you like this?" Detective Palmer asked Malaysia while they gazed in my direction.

"No, I don't have any enemies," she said.

"Then maybe this attempt on your life wasn't meant for you at all, Miss Hughes. I mean, if you heard them say kill that nigga, you probably weren't the intended target," Detective Ashford said.

"What are you saying?" she asked.

"The truck is registered to Mr. Clark, right?" Detective Palmer inquired.

"Yea, so…"

"So, maybe it was him that they were after and you just got caught in the middle. I mean, as dark as the tint on that truck is, no one could know for certain who was in the truck. So, Mr. Clark who is it that wants you dead?" Detective Ashford asked me.

"You don't know that they were after me and neither do I. I suggest you continue questioning Malaysia, so you can get the fuck on outta here, and she can get some rest," I said eyeing the man evilly.

"I knew it! I knew yo ass had something to do with my child lying up in this fuckin' hospital bed! Can't you arrest his ass for that shit?" Louise asked as she gave me the evil eyes.

"No ma'am, without any proof of any wrongdoings, we cannot arrest him. But if you know anything that can help us, please let us know. He is under investigation for the death of his previous girlfriend and we'll be investigating the incident involving your daughter. If you can think of anything, please give us a call," Detective Ashford said as he handed her a card.

"Hellllllloooooo! I'm standing right here and y'all gonna act like I'm not even in the fuckin' room. Malaysia, I'ma hit you up later because who doesn't have time for this bullshit is me!" I said.

I didn't have time for that shit, so I pushed past those fucking clowns and out the door. I pushed the down button for the elevator and waited for it to come get me. When the car stopped at my floor, I didn't hesitate to jump in. As I rode down, I thought about what the detectives said. I knew they questioned me when Alize's body was found, so I knew I was a suspect. But it's been months since her body turned up, so I had no idea that I was under investigation.

They were trying to pin her death on me, but they wouldn't be able to. Even though I did it, I felt like I was well within my rights. Roz said that Alize was planning a surprise birthday party for me with my dad. I needed to speak to my mom about that because even if she was helping him put a party together for me, that didn't explain what she was doing under his desk between his legs.

I didn't care what that hoe said; Alize was sucking my dad's dick and they all deserved what they got. A few days after Roz went missing, there was a missing person's report filed because her family hadn't heard from her.

They could be searching for Roz for years and would never find her ass; I made sure of that shit. I jumped in my car and headed to my mom's house to question her about this supposed surprise party. No one had mentioned it to me, so why would I take the word of a whore instead of going with what I know I saw. She tried to explain to me that it wasn't what I thought, but I wasn't trying to hear that shit because the eyes didn't lie.

*****

Thirty minutes later I was pulling up in front of my mom's brownstone. I walked in and went in search of my mom. The first place I looked was the kitchen because that was where she normally was. I was right; she was whipping up some muffins when I walked in.

"Hey ma," I said, startling her.

"Princeton! I didn't hear you come in. What you doing here and how is Malaysia feeling?" she asked.

"She's better. Her mom and the police were there when I left," I said.

"Do they know who shot up your truck?" she asked.

"Nah, they think that whoever did it might have been trying to hit me."

"Princeton!" she said as she gasped and clutched her chest. "Do you think those bullets were meant for you?" She had a worried expression on her face as she waited to hear my answer.

"Yea mom, I think so. I mean, who would want to hurt Malaysia that way? And she was driving my truck, so yea, I think somebody wants me dead," I said honestly.

In the business I was in, I did a lot of ruthless things to get where I was. But, when you were a boss like me, there were things that you had to do to maintain that boss status. So, if that meant you had to take out a few bad apples, then that was what needed to be done. It made no sense to hold on to people who would only bring you down.

"Son, I worry about you and Zay so much, just as I used to worry about your dad. You have to be careful because I already lost your dad. I would hate to lose you guys too," she said.

Did she say she would hate to lose me and Zay like my dad? What the fuck! I was her son, her only son, so why was she worried about that lil nigga? I never understood my mom. That young boy was fucking my little sister and instead of wanting him dead, she was worried he might end up dead. Well, if I had anything to do with it, he would definitely meet his maker real soon.

"Zay? Why the hell you worried about that nigga? He ain't yo son! Matter of fact, he ain't shit to you!" I said angrily.

"Watch your tone when you're talking to me, boy! I done told you about coming in my house trying to disrespect me," she said as she waved her finger all up in my face.

"I'm sorry, ma. I didn't mean to disrespect you. But hearing that you are worried about that nigga when he ain't a member of this family pisses me off!" I said.

"He is a member of this family, for your information," she said.

"Ma, just because you take in a stray does not make them family."

"Wow! A stray, huh? I don't know what has gotten into you that would make you treat Zay like that after all he has done for this family. He has done nothing but protect and provide for our family, just like your father used to do. What is your issue with him?" she asked.

"I told you, he crossed the line when he disregarded my warnings to stay away from Lexus. It was like he thought I was some kind of joke or something. I mean, how hard was it for him to just leave her alone. Where is she anyway?" I asked.

"Your sister is at her house," she simply said as she put her muffins in the oven.

"Her what?" I asked, knowing damn well she didn't say what I thought I heard.

"Her house," she repeated.

"I wasn't asking about Ja'Kyra. I was asking where Lexus is. Is she upstairs?" I asked.

"No son and I was speaking of Lexus. Zay asked your sister to marry him and she said yes. The two of them are engaged now and he bought them a beautiful home. So, she moved in with her fiancé," my mom said.

"Wait, what! You cannot be serious, ma! You not only let her date the dude, but you let her get engaged and move in with that punk?" I asked.

I was livid! I mean, what kind of mother allowed her 18-year old daughter to not only move in with some young punk, but get engaged to him also? What the hell was going on with my mom? It was almost like since dad died, she just didn't care what we did anymore. My sister, Ja'Kyra was living with her boyfriend and now Lexus was engaged to marry that punk, Zay. Well, it was time to put a stop to this nonsense. They would live together and get married over my dead body.

"Wait a minute, in case you haven't noticed, your sister is a grown woman and she doesn't need you or me telling her what to do like she's still a little kid. She loves Zay and he loves her. I don't understand what the big deal about their relationship is to you or why it is any of your concern. I think you just need to let this go!" she said.

"It is my concern because dad isn't around anymore, so I'm in charge. Who else is going to look out for the family if not me?" I asked.

"Oh wow! So that's what you're doing? You're looking out for the family?" she asked with a smirk on her face. I didn't know what had gotten into my mom. She had never behaved so stubbornly when my dad was alive. Why couldn't she see that Zay was not the man for Lexus?

"What is that supposed to mean?" I asked.

"Well, how much have you really done to help this family since your father was killed? I mean, you didn't help pay for the funeral, not one dime. Then, you showed up to the funeral drunk and high. So, please tell me what you have done for your family lately?" she asked with her hand on her hip.

"I've been here mom, but this hasn't been easy for me either, ya know? I lost my dad too and my girlfriend, so it has been harder for me than any of you. All I want is a little respect and support from my family, but do I get that? No!" I said.

I was sick and tired of them acting like I didn't belong in this damn family. With my dad being gone, that left me as head honcho in charge, so they needed to recognize that shit and stay in line.

"Why are you here? Just tell me what it is that you need because I don't feel like continuing this discussion. You'll never see things from anyone else's perspective but your own, so what's up?" she asked.

"I almost forgot why I even came here. I needed to know if you knew anything about a surprise party that was being planned for my birthday," I said.

"Yea. Me, your dad, and Alize were working on it. Alize wanted to do something special for you and she thought a surprise birthday party was the answer. She had gone to get money from your dad to pay for the venue a couple of days before they found her body. I didn't even know she was missing," my mom said.

"Well, we did have a falling out and she left. I just figured that she went to her mom's house to cool off. Her cousin Roz said she was planning a surprise party for me, but I didn't know," I said, feeling like shit all of a sudden.

"Well, of course you didn't know, otherwise it wouldn't have been a surprise."

"I gotta go," I said and headed for the door.

All I wanted to know was if Alize was planning a surprise party for me and now that I had this information, I felt like shit. How could I have not trusted her? How could I have thought she was sleeping with my dad? I felt sick to my stomach, but I wasn't about to let my mom see me sweat.

I jumped in my truck and headed to the warehouse to see what those muthafuckas was up to. On the ride there, I had to pull over and throw up. I took several deep breaths as my eyes flooded with tears. I wasn't going to cry over this shit.

"FUUUUUCCCKKKK!" I yelled as I hit the steering wheel. That was the first time I got that emotional over Alize's death. I wished I had known what she and my parents were up to. If I had known, none of that shit would have happened.

Well, what was done was done and there wasn't any use crying like a bitch over it. I wiped the tears that were threatening to fall and got back on the road, heading to the warehouse. I had about six of my men that had gone missing in the past four weeks, which was stressing me out. Not to mention the attempt on Malaysia's life, so I wondered what the hell was going on.

Who the fuck was out to get me? If I found out that it was Zay, so help me God!

CHAPTER NINE

Lexus

Two Months Later...

My baby girl was due in two weeks and I was beyond excited. I still hadn't seen my brother since I found out that information, but I had way too much going on to worry about him now. It seemed like everything was going the way I wanted it to, but I always kept my guard up.

Just when I thought things were going great, things had a way of switching up. Zay and I found out about our baby girl when we went to my five-month checkup. I couldn't be more excited to be having a little girl. I would have been just as happy if we had found out we were having a son. I just wanted our baby to be healthy. We decided to name our baby girl Za'Nya Michelle and I couldn't wait to meet her.

The day we found out we were having a girl we went shopping for baby furniture and other things to decorate the nursery. We went with pink and lavender colors and white furniture. By the time we were done decorating the nursery, it was absolutely beautiful. My mom and sisters had come by to help us get everything set up. Chico and Chance had also dropped by with their ladies, so we just decided to have a party. The guys lit up the grill while us ladies cooked on the inside.

Today we had an appointment with the doctor since the baby was due in a couple of weeks. I woke up this morning, excited about my visit to the doctor. It didn't take long for that feeling of excitement to be replaced with pain.

My lower back began to hurt like crazy, but I tried my best not to reveal those feelings to Zay because I didn't want him to be worried. I figured it was Braxton Hicks contractions anyway, so there was no need for him to be running around all crazy for nothing.

I put on my pink Donna Morgan maternity dress and slipped into my Jimmy Choo sandals and went to wait for my man to come and scoop me up. He had left early this morning to go handle some business, so I sat and waited for him to come back. My appointment was at 11:00 a.m. and it was already ten, so if he wasn't here within the next ten minutes, I was going to give him a call.

As I walked to the living room, I had another cramp. I grabbed my back and practiced the breathing techniques we learned in child birthing classes. After a couple of minutes, the pain subsided. By that time, Zay was walking through door.

"Hey baby, you ready?" he asked.

"Yep," I said as I stood up and grabbed my handbag.

He gave me a kiss and we walked out together. He opened the door for me, and I slipped in the smooth buttery seats. He walked around to the driver's side and got behind the wheel. He started the car and it came to life with a purr. He backed out the driveway and jumped on the highway, heading to the doctor's office.

I must have made a face that exhibited the kind of pain I was experiencing because he grabbed my hand and asked, "You okay?"

"Yea," I lied. "I'm fine."

"Stop lying. I know you too well for you to sit there and tell me a damn lie. What's wrong?" he asked with a serious look on his face.

I looked at him and said, "I woke up with a little pain in my lower back, that's all. But we're on our way to the doctor, so I didn't want to worry you."

"Baby, why didn't you call me, so I could take you in sooner?" he asked, looking worried.

That's exactly what I didn't want to happen.

"Because I don't think it's all that serious. I think it may be Braxton Hicks or something. I didn't want to bother you because I knew you had things to do. I'll be fine," I said.

"How are you feeling now?" he asked.

"I feel okay and the pains only last a little while then go away," I said.

"How long has this been going on?"

"For a couple of hours," I said as I gripped his hand because of another cramp.

"Well, we're almost there, so you need to let them know as soon as we walk in how you been feeling," he said.

"I will babe, stop worrying," I said.

We pulled into the parking lot 15 minutes later and he parked the car. He made his way around to help me out of the car. I was glad we were here because these pains were really starting to hurt.

"Thank God we're here because these Braxton Hicks ain't no joke," I said as we walked into the doctor's office. It hurt so much to walk. I felt as if my pussy was about to explode.

I sat in the chair closest to the door while I continued to do my breathing exercises. Zay walked up to the receptionist's desk and said, "My fiancée has an eleven o'clock appointment, but she's been in a lot of pain all morning. She needs to be seen like right now."

"Let's get her to an examination room, so we can get her checked out. Miss Clark, can you follow me to the back?" she asked.

Zay came to help me to my feet and we followed Erica to the exam room.

"Remove your panties and drape this over your bottom half. I will go get Dr. Langley," Erica said as she walked out of the room.

I did as she instructed and slowly sat on the table. My body was in so much pain, but I tried to remain calm. Zay sat beside me and rubbed my back as I breathed in and out the way I was taught.

Dr. Langley knocked on the door and walked in. She took one look at me and asked, "How long have you been feeling this way?" She slipped on her gloves and told me to lie down on the exam table. I leaned back, and she began to do a pelvic exam, which was just as uncomfortable as the pains.

"Oh my! You're in labor!" the doctor informed us.

"What?!" Zay and I exclaimed at the same time.

"Yes ma'am, you are at seven centimeters dilated," she said in her rich Malaysian accent.

"Oh my God! Zay, call my mom please," I said as my anxiety shot through the roof.

"Hold on, Zay. Before you do that, I'm going to need you to take her to the hospital right now. I'll meet you there within the next 20 minutes," Dr. Langley said.

"Am I gonna last that long?" I asked nervously.

"Yes, you should be fine until I get there. I'll call the hospital and let them know that you are coming in, so they can prep and get you ready for delivery. I promise you that I am gonna be right behind you. Can you walk to the car or do you need a wheelchair?" the doctor asked.

"No, I think I can walk out," I said.

"Okay, I'll go and let my staff know that I'll be out of the office. Then I'll be on my way to the hospital," she said.

"Okay, Dr. Langley, thank you," Zay said.

"You're welcome. Lexus keep doing your breathing techniques because they do help," the doctor advised.

I just nodded my head because I was in the middle of one of those breathing techniques at that very moment. Once she left the room, I slid off the table so Zay and I could head to the hospital. On the way there, my pains became excruciating. I had heard a lot of stories about the pain of childbirth, but I never imagined it would feel anything like this. Zay called my mom like I asked so she could meet us there.

As soon as we arrived at the hospital, I was whisked away to my room with Zay in tow. I was given a hospital gown to put on as I doubled over in pain. Zay and I went into the bathroom, so I could change into it. When we were done, we headed back into the room and I slid in the comfortable hospital bed.

"Is it too late for me to get an epidural?" I asked.

"We need to check your cervix before we can make that determination," said the nurse.

"Well, can you hurry please; these pains are killing me."

"Let me connect your IV and the baby monitor, then I'll get the doctor on duty," the nurse said.

As she prepared to put the IV in my arm, I shied away because I hated needles. Zay held my hand and comforted me as I winced in pain. Right after she was finished putting the IV in my arm, my mom came busting in the hospital room. She strapped the monitor around my swollen belly, and we could hear the baby's heartbeat, loud and clear. I smiled as I heard how strong her little heartbeat was. I couldn't wait to hold her in my arms.

"Baby are you okay?" my mom asked as she rushed over to me.

"Yea, just in a lot of pain," I said.

"You didn't get your epidural yet?" my mom asked.

"No, she said they have to check my cervix first," I said.

"Well, where the heck is your doctor? She needs to come in here and do her damn job!" my mom said.

"Ma'am, I was just about to buzz for her," the nurse said.

"Well, hurry up!" my mom said.

"I need to check her cervix first," the nurse said.

"Well, what the hell are you waiting for?" my mom asked. My mom was such a firecracker and people wondered why I was the way that I was. My mom didn't take any shit and neither did I.

The nurse pulled up the seat as I placed my feet in the stirrups. She stuck her fingers in my kitty, which caused me to be even more uncomfortable. She pulled her hand back and said, "I'll be right back."

She removed her gloves and tossed them in the trash as she hurried out of the room. My mom went to the bathroom and returned to the room with a wet towel. She placed the cold cloth on my forehead.

"I know that this doesn't help much, but at least it can keep you cool," my mom said.

Dr. Langley walked into the room a short time later and greeted us before she put on her latex gloves. She checked my cervix and said, "I'm sorry Lexus, but you are too far to receive an epidural."

"What do you mean she's too far?" my mom asked.

"She's ten centimeters," Dr. Langley informed us.

"But her water didn't even break. Isn't her water supposed to break?" Zay asked.

"Lexus is in active labor, so this baby is coming. Okay Lexus, I know you're in pain, but I'm going to need you to push when I tell you to. Okay?" she asked.

"Wait! I'm having the baby right now?" I asked as all my nerves kicked in. I couldn't have the baby right now. I wasn't ready.

"Yes, so get ready to push on this next contraction," she said. All I could do was nod my head in understanding. I couldn't believe I was in active labor and I wouldn't be getting any relief for the pain. Oh my God! The shit hurt so bad.

Zay held one hand and my mom held my other one as the nurses held my legs up and open.

"Okay Lexus, I need you to take a deep breath and push until I count to ten. Okay, push! One, two, three, four, five, six, seven, eight, nine, ten! Okay, breathe. I can see your baby girl's head. You're doing really good," Dr. Langley praised.

"I love you so much," Zay said as he kissed my hand.

"It hurts," I said.

"I know baby, but you're almost there," he said.

"Okay Lexus, I need you to push again until I count to ten. Take a deep breath and bear down. Push! One, two, three, four, five, six, seven, eight, nine, ten. Okay, breathe. You're doing great Lexus! One more push and your baby will be in your arms," the doctor said.

"You're doing great, baby," my mom said with a smile.

"Yea, you really are," Zay said.

"Okay Lexus, I'm going to need you to push one more time. Deep breath, bear down, and push! One, two, three, four, five, six, seven, eight, nine, ten! And she's here!" Dr. Langley announced.

Soon after she made that statement, I heard the most beautiful sound I had ever heard. My baby girl was finally here, and I couldn't have been a happier mommy. A couple of seconds after the doctor announced her arrival, we heard the shrill of her cries and then she was placed on my stomach. She had the most beautiful eyes, a perfect little nose like her daddy, and a head full of curly black hair. She was absolutely beautiful, and I fell in love with her at first sight.

"She's beautiful!" I cried.

"Yes, she is," my mom said.

I looked over at Zay, who had a single tear rolling down his cheek. This was the first time I had ever seen my man show this much emotion. He looked at me and then at our baby with such amazement in his eyes.

He leaned down and kissed my lips. "Thank you."

"Thank you," I responded back to him.

"Okay, let's finish this up while they take the baby and get her cleaned up and weighed," Doctor Langley said.

The nurse removed the baby from her resting place, which caused her to start crying. I wanted to tell her to bring my baby back to me, but I knew that she needed to get cleaned and weighed. I began to feel those cramps again and knew I needed to push out the placenta. I had read several books about delivering a baby because I wanted to make sure that everything went according to what I read and knew.

"Okay Lexus, I need you to push, but not as hard as you pushed for your baby," Dr. Langley said.

I began to lightly push until I felt the release of the placenta, then I leaned back against the bed. I was so glad that this was over. When I imagined giving birth, I imagined it going a whole different way. I imagined being in La La Land after receiving my epidural. I never dreamed that I would have to push out my baby girl without any medication whatsoever.

The nurse returned with our little bundle, all wrapped in her blanket with her snug little cap. She turned to Zay and asked, "Would you like to hold your daughter?"

"Oh yes, ma'am," he said as he reached out for the nurse to put the baby in his arms.

I watched as the love of my life held our precious Za'Nya for the first time and tears sprang to my own eyes. I felt my mom's hand on mine and she whispered, "You did good, baby girl."

"Thanks mommy," I smiled as she kissed my forehead.

"Your baby girl weighs six pounds and two ounces, and she is 18 inches long," the nurse said.

"She's perfect," I said as I watched Zay with tears in his eyes. I knew right then that I had made the right decision to be with him. I knew that he would always make sure that we were good. My heart swelled as I watched my man with our baby girl.

CHAPTER TEN

Malaysia

I had been released from the hospital a month and a half ago. I was now living with my mom because she refused to let me go back to Princeton. I wasn't even sure if I wanted to go back home with him anyway. I was now seven and a half months pregnant with a baby boy and the last thing I needed was stress from him. I prayed that my baby looked like me and not Anthony since I had told Princeton that this was his baby. He came to the hospital when I was released to take me to his place, but I didn't want to go with him.

I was more than sure what happened to me that day was just me being in the wrong place at the wrong time. I had spoken to the detectives and I knew that the bullets they rained down on me were meant for Princeton. He didn't want me to go with my mom, but since she had also arrived at the hospital to get me, he decided not to pick a fight.

While I was here, he called several times wanting me to come back, but I wouldn't go. I couldn't risk getting shot at again, especially not while I was pregnant. I was so close to having my baby that I wasn't about to risk his little life behind Princeton's mess. I had already lost one baby, so I wasn't about to lose another one. I felt comfortable at my mom's house because I knew no one would try to kill me here. Anthony had been by a few times, but I turned him away every time.

My mom felt that he and I should talk, especially once I told her that he was the father of my baby and not Princeton. She was so happy that Princeton wasn't the father because he had put my life in danger. She knew that he lived a dangerous life and didn't want him around my baby. I was sitting in the living room watching television when there was a knock at the door. I waited to see if my mom would answer it, but she didn't.

I opened the door and there stood Princeton. I thought I was safe here and that he wouldn't come here, especially since he knew how my mom felt about him. I guess I underestimated him and should have known that he had more balls than to let my mom dictate anything to him.

"What are you doing here?" I asked.

"I came for you. I need to take you back home, so we can prepare for our baby together," he said with a smile.

"I'm not going back with you. I told you before that I was staying here."

He reached out and touched my stomach. I pulled back, but he continued to rub my belly with one hand while pulling me close with the other. I tried to move away from him, but he began to kiss my neck, which always drove me crazy. He nibbled on my earlobes while he continued to rub my swollen belly.

"You wanna make love to me, don't you?" he whispered in my ear as he stroked my back.

I couldn't even answer because I was feeling so good. He knew how to get me and at that moment, I was at a loss for words. The only thing that could be heard from me was the moans that I directed towards him.

"You want me, don't you?" he asked.

Oh God, yessssss! I screamed inside my head.

"Wouldn't you like to know?" I said seductively to him.

"I already know you miss me. And I know you want this dick all up in that fat, pregnant pussy of yours," he said as he ran a hand up my thighs until he found my panties that were dripping wet.

"You're so wet," he said as he kissed me.

I didn't want to give in to him, but my body missed him. My pussy wanted to feel him inside me. Princeton had made love to me like no other man I had ever been with. He touched spots that I didn't even know I had, and he had awakened a beast in me that I never knew was there.

"Go get your things baby, and come home," he whispered.

Noooooooooo! my mind screamed.

"I'll be right back," I said as he stood in the front hallway of our house.

I went to my bedroom and grabbed my stuff and went to find my mom, but I didn't have to look far. I heard her screaming for Princeton to leave her house.

"GET THE FUCK OUT OF MY HOUSE! YOU ARE NO LONGER WELCOME HERE!" she yelled at him.

He had his back turned and was getting ready to open the front door when I called after him. "Princeton wait!"

"Where are you going?" my mom asked.

"I'm going home, mom."

"You are home, Malaysia!" she said.

"No mom, my home is with Princeton and I just need you to accept that," I said, hoping that she wouldn't mention the fact that my baby was not his.

"I will never accept that. This man almost got you killed, and you're going to go back and live with him? Why?" she asked.

"Because I love him, and he loves me," I said as he laced his fingers with mine and took my bag.

"He doesn't love you. All he cares about is himself and what he wants. Don't do this, don't go with him. Stay here where you'll be safe," my mom begged.

I almost changed my mind because she looked so broken. The last thing I wanted to do was hurt my mom. I loved my mom so much, but I had to do this for myself.

"I'll be fine, mom. You worry too much," I said.

"I won't let anyone hurt her," Princeton said.

"You're the one that keeps hurting her. I don't know what kind of hold you have on my child, but I swear if you hurt my daughter or she turns up missing, I'll make sure you go to jail for the rest of your miserable fuckin' life," my mom said to Princeton while clenching her teeth.

"I'm not trying to hurt your daughter and if I were you, I would definitely watch out for those threats. You never know when those words you speak can come back to haunt your ass," he said.

"Are you threatening me? Are you threatening me, muthafucka?" my mom asked.

"Mom, he didn't threaten you. All he said was watch how you talk to people. Now, I'll see you in a couple of days," I said.

"Don't go with him, Malaysia. Please stay with me, honey. I'm so scared for you. Don't you know that you aren't safe with him! Please stay here with me." My mom pleaded with tears in her eyes.

The look on her face was so frightened as she spoke those words. I felt the urge to stay with her, but my pussy was dripping to feel Princeton's dick inside of me. I turned to my mom and said, "I'll be fine, mom. I'll see you in a couple of days. I love you."

"I love you too." She said as she pulled me into her arms for a hug and kissed me on the cheek.

As I turned to leave, I knew I was breaking my mom's heart, but I couldn't help it. The heart wanted what the heart wanted, and the pussy wanted what the pussy wanted. As I descended the steps, I turned to wave at my mom, who was standing in the doorway crying.

I would see her in a couple of days and hopefully, things would be okay. If I knew then that I would never see my mother alive again, I would have stayed with her. I wished I could turn back the hands of time.

*****

When Princeton and I got to his place, we wasted no time getting naked and falling in bed. He pushed me back on the bed and got down between my legs, sucking and licking my wet spot. I hadn't felt his tongue in over a month, so that shit felt so good. I was literally bouncing off the walls as he ate me like my pussy was a Thanksgiving turkey.

I came three times in less than 15 minutes, and he licked and slurped it all up, not leaving a drop behind. I was practically begging for him to put his dick inside me. He climbed between my legs and thrust his dick deep inside me, causing me to shudder and cream on his dick from the sheer bliss of what I was feeling.

I couldn't believe how wonderful I felt right now. He kissed me hungrily and I kissed him back. I was just as hungry for him as he was for me and I had to admit that I did miss my man. He pushed his dick deeper inside me and I thought I was gonna lose my mind.

"Let me get in that kitty cat from the back," he said.

I turned over and positioned myself comfortably as he prepared to hit it from behind. When he shoved his dick inside me, I shuddered again. He held my hips and pounded me hard from behind. I didn't think I could take it like that because of the baby, but I wasn't going to stop him because it felt good. The only problem I had was trying not to hurt my shoulder, which still had some sore muscles from the shooting.

He smacked my ass and held my hips tighter as he grinded his pelvis into me. Damn! That felt good. Finally, he succumbed to his orgasmic feelings and we came at the same time. If I wouldn't have been pregnant already, this would have definitely sealed the deal on a pregnancy. I laid in bed next to him until he got a phone call.

"Waddup," he answered.

He was quiet for a minute and then he left to take the call in another room. I didn't follow or try to be nosey because I was worn out. I just laid in bed, rubbing my belly which seemed to be growing by the day. I marveled at the sight as I watched my son rumbling and tumbling inside my belly.

Princeton returned 15 minutes later with a bottle of water and a glass of milk. He handed me the glass of milk and opened the bottle of water. He sat on the edge of the bed as I watched his body glistening with sweat from our afternoon romp.

"You aight?" he asked.

"Yea, better than ever," I said, smiling as I drank the milk. I didn't really like milk too much, but it was a healthy drink for the baby, so…

"I gotta go see my sister, but I'll be back in a couple of hours," he said as he walked to the bathroom and turned on the water.

"Can I come?" I asked, anxious to see Zay.

I knew he was talking about Lexus because I had heard through the grapevine that she had her baby. I could care less about her or her little brat; I just wanted to see her man. I couldn't get over the fact that Zay had the best dick I had ever been served. It surprised me that I was still craving his dick after getting all the dick I could want from Princeton. I only had sex with Zay once, but I still wanted him. I craved him. I wanted to feel him inside me again, to feel my knees weaken from the dick down, and to kiss his lips.

"I don't think that would be a good idea. You and my sister have been at odds for a while. Why don't y'all get along anymore anyway? Y'all two used to be so close," he said.

"Yea, I know. As I told you before, I think we just grew apart. But just because we don't hang like we used to doesn't mean I don't care for her. In my mind, she'll always be my best friend. I just wanna see her and let her know how happy I am for her," I lied.

Truth was I didn't give a shit about Lexus. The only reason I wanted to go was because I knew that Zay would be by her side at the hospital. I waited for Princeton to give me the okay before I got dressed.

"Okay, but I don't want you starting shit," he warned.

"I don't want to start any shit. I just want to see her baby girl. After all, our babies will be growing up together, so we may as well squash this beef since they'll be seeing a lot of each other," I said.

"You're right."

He made his way to the bathroom and I followed him. I may as well take a shower with him, so we could finish faster. The sooner we could finish taking a shower and getting dressed, the sooner we could go so I could see Zay's sexy ass. I had taken a picture of Zay at Big Jim's funeral when no one was watching and every so often, I would just stare at it and imagine that he was mine.

I stepped in the shower behind Princeton and began to lather myself as he washed himself. This was probably the first time we had taken a shower together and didn't have sex. Every time we got in the shower, it was followed by some hot sex, but I was a woman on a mission. That being said, sex was the last thing I was looking for, at least from Princeton. If Zay wanted it, he could damn sure get it.

We finished up and got dressed. We hopped in his Mercedes E Class Coupe and jumped on the highway headed to the hospital. I sat there listening to the smooth sounds of Chris Brown while rubbing my belly. I began to hum, and my little man began to do flip flops in my stomach. I grabbed Princeton's hand and placed it on my stomach, so he could feel the baby move. His eyes opened in amazement as he felt my baby boy move around.

"He's pretty strong, huh?" he asked with a huge smile on his face.

"Yep, just like his daddy." I smiled back.

"I can't wait to hold my little man. I'm so excited that we're having a boy," he beamed.

"Yea, I can't wait to meet him either."

The rest of the ride was quiet. I wasn't sure what he was thinking about, but the only thing I had on my mind was seeing Zay.

*****

Finally, we arrived at the hospital and Princeton found a parking spot in no time. We walked hand in hand inside the hospital and headed toward the elevator.

"Princeton, don't you think we should get her a gift for the baby?" I asked as we passed up the gift shop.

"Yea, that's a good idea," he said as we went inside.

We looked around until we found a little pink stuffed elephant with some little pink booties on its feet. We also bought some pink and white roses and some balloons. He picked out this big Mylar balloon that looked like a pink baby bottle with the words 'It's a Girl' on it. He spent almost a hundred dollars for these gifts, and I was happy I had suggested it. It would definitely look good when we walked in carrying all these gifts.

We got in the elevator and pressed the third-floor button. My nerves were really bundled as we got closer to seeing Zay. The elevator dinged which let us know that we had reached our designated floor. We walked out of the elevator and headed to the nurse's station.

We knew what floor Lexus was on, but we didn't know what room. After finding out that she was in room 305, we headed that way. When we reached the room, I took a deep breath and followed behind Princeton.

When we walked in, Lexus was sitting up in bed and Zay was sitting next to her holding their baby. I immediately saw red because that should have been our baby. I was pregnant by Zay first, so that should have been our baby he was holding.

I calmed down and plastered a fake smile on my face while my heart beat erratically, it could have given me a stroke. I don't know why I still wanted Zay, but I did. I looked at him as he held his baby girl and he was the perfect dad, just as I knew he would be.

"Hey y'all," Princeton said, snapping me back into the present.

"Hey," Lexus and Zay greeted us. They definitely did not look happy to see us. It didn't matter though because I was too happy to see Zay. I was so happy, in fact, I almost pissed on myself.

"We just came by to see my niece and to bring you these," Princeton said as we put the gifts on the table next to all her other gifts. I'm sure Zay had purchased most of them because he was excited about their baby.

"Thank you," Lexus said as she kept her face stoic. I wondered what the fuck she had up her ass. I mean, she just had a baby, so she should have been happier than she actually was. They both looked as if they had something stuck up their asses.

While Lexus said thank you, Zay didn't bother to say anything as he stared at Princeton. If you asked me, he looked angry as fuck that we were there. But I didn't give a shit. I was on cloud nine looking at him, with his handsome self.

"How's your little Princess doing?" Princeton asked with an awkward smile on his face.

"She's perfect. How did you know we were here?" Lexus asked.

"We sorta heard it through the grapevine, ya know? My little sister had a baby and no one in the family bothered to even tell me," Princeton said.

"Well, it ain't like we been on the best of terms," Lexus said.

"Yea, I know," Princeton said as he turned his gaze over to Zay. "Can I hold her?"

Zay looked at Lexus, who had this weird smirk on her face. It was almost as if she didn't want her own brother to hold her baby. What was going on with them? I knew there was some tension between them about Lexus and Zay getting together, but damn! The tension in the room was so thick, you could cut it with a knife.

"Yea, sure," Zay said as he walked over to Princeton with the baby girl in his arms. He slipped her into Princeton's arms and said, "Be careful with her head."

"I know man. This ain't my first time holding a baby," Princeton said. He stood there holding the baby and looking at her so intently. "She's so beautiful. What's her name?"

"Za'Nya," Zay said as he stood watch over his baby girl. I didn't care why he was standing near us, just the scent of him had my pussy wet. I resented Lexus for being with him and giving him the life that I should have had with him. I had him first. I was pregnant by him first. She took him from me, and I wanted him back.

"Malaysia, you are getting big, girl. When are you due?" Lexus asked. Her tone sounded friendly, but her facial expression told it all. She definitely wasn't happy that we had barged in on their family time.

"In about six weeks," I said.

"Are you nervous?" she asked.

"Not really. I'm more anxious than I am nervous. I'm just ready to hold my baby boy," I said.

I had a fake smile on my face just the way she had on hers. I had been holding mine for so long, I prayed the good Lord wouldn't freeze it like that. When Lexus pushed a strand of hair behind her left ear and I saw the huge rock on her finger, I almost fainted.

I literally vomited in my mouth and started gagging. Now, I had heard about the baby, but the ring… that was something I didn't know. I had no idea that they were engaged, so that took me by surprise and almost knocked me off my feet.

"You aight?" Princeton asked as he looked at me.

"Yea, I'm fine." I wasn't fine though. I felt as if God was punishing me for something because he kept dealing me all these bad hands. "That is a beautiful ring!"

"Oh, thank you." Lexus beamed as she stared at the rock on her left hand. "Zay and I got engaged about three months ago. He is such a romantic that he enlisted the help of my mom and sisters. It was so perfect!" she said as they kissed each other.

"Wow! Well, congratulations!" I managed to say around the lump in my throat.

"Thank you!" she and Zay said at the same time.

I looked over at Princeton, who wasn't even paying attention to anything or anyone else except the baby he held. I walked over to where he was now sitting because I wanted to see the baby. She was perfect. She had a pretty little nose like Zay's and her little pouty lips were too cute. I almost cried as I looked at the baby that Lexus had for Zay. I was supposed to have his baby. That was supposed to be my fucking ring!

I smiled nervously and said, "I'll be right back."

I had to excuse myself from the room because if I stayed there one more minute, I was going to lose it. I rushed to the public restroom on the second floor and went into the stall. I cried, screamed, and even kicked the door a couple of times.

"Are you okay?" someone asked from outside the stall.

"Mind your own fuckin' business!" I yelled.

I was so upset that all I saw was red. I had to remember that I was pregnant and couldn't get too excited because I didn't want to hurt the baby. I took several deep breaths to calm myself down. I walked out of the stall and made my way to the sink. I splashed some water on my face in an effort to bring myself back to normal. After I did that, I stared at my reflection in the mirror.

Looking at me, you would never guess that I had so much anger inside me. I looked like a normal pregnant woman, but that just went to show that looks could be deceiving. I wasn't normal. I was an angry black woman and those two put together were not a good combination.

I took another deep breath before I opened the door. I headed back upstairs, hoping that Princeton would be ready to go once I got there. I couldn't take that shit anymore. Why couldn't I be happy with Zay? Why wasn't I enough woman for him?

CHAPTER ELEVEN

Princeton

I had to come and visit my little sister. I mean, she did just give birth to my niece. That alone had me wired and pissed the fuck off. Lexus was only 18 years old. What the fuck did she know about being a mother? I pushed all those ill feelings I had and mustered up the courage to go see her and my niece but seeing her with Zay literally had my blood boiling. I knew that she was happy, and I should put that beef behind me, but I couldn't. Seeing my little niece made me think about when my baby girl was first born. She was absolutely beautiful.

I watched Lexus and Zay together and they looked really happy but fuck that shit. I had given that nigga specific warnings to stay away from my sister and he chose to ignore them. That was some disrespectful shit. I didn't know anyone in the hood that would just be able to get over that shit. I knew I couldn't, no matter how hard I tried.

I didn't know where Malaysia went, but I knew when she got back, I was ready to go. I wasn't concerned about where she went as I held my beautiful niece in my arms. Watching Zay and Lexus together made me want to throw him out that fucking window. How the fuck he gonna propose to my little sister and why the hell would my mom and sisters help him? It was almost as if everybody had gone wild and I was the only sane one left.

When Zay kissed my little sister with me standing right there, I was like what the fuck! This nigga just disrespected me right to my damn face.

Once Malaysia brought her ass back from wherever, we said our goodbyes. I kissed my sister on the cheek and gave Za'Nya a kiss on the forehead. I watched Malaysia give my sister a hug, then kiss the baby on the forehead and move towards Zay. I watched as she gave him a hug, which in my opinion lasted a little too long.

I held onto her waist as we walked to the elevator together. I was hoping to receive a text message from my boy letting me know the favor I asked him for was done. I looked at my watch and it was only 6:45 PM, so I realized it was too early for that to happen.

When Malaysia and I got to the car, I asked, "Are you hungry?"

"You know I'm eating for two, so I'm always hungry," she said with a smile on her pretty face as she rubbed her stomach.

"Yea, you are definitely eating for two," I said.

We got in the car and I revved up the engine. I loved this fucking car, even though I didn't always drive it. I probably didn't drive it as much because of how much I loved it. I didn't like scratches, dents, or anything fucking with my ride. I hadn't had the chance to replace my truck yet, but I would. I was actually waiting on a Harley Davidson truck to come into the dealership.

"What you feel like eating?" I asked.

"I feel like eating pizza. Can we go to Gino's?" she asked with a smile on her face.

"Hell yea, we can go to Gino's! I love their pizza and pasta!"

So, I headed over to Gino's where I hoped to eat until I burst. I looked over at Malaysia as she sat and rubbed her belly. She had been doing that a lot lately and I must admit, I was happy that she was pregnant. I couldn't wait for her to have our son.

"What do you think about naming our baby Prince?" I asked.

"Prince? Is that your way of saying you want to name our baby Princeton Jr.?" she asked.

"Well, I would be lying if I said that wasn't one of the reasons, I'm so happy we're having a boy. I have always wanted a baby to carry on my family name."

"Well, don't think you will be introducing our son into that crazy drug life you lead. I know how happy you are about our son, but I won't have him involved in anything to do with drugs," she said.

"Are you kidding me right now? Our baby isn't even born yet and you're warning me to keep him away from drugs. That's a low blow, don't you think?"

I never once thought anything like that. My son would be my pride and joy, just like my daughter. There was no way I wanted either of my children anywhere near the warehouse. I would shield them away from that part of my life for as long as I could. That was just something that they didn't need to know about.

When we arrived at Gino's, we were seated right away. I was starving, and I needed to kill some time while I waited for things to go down tonight.

"Hello, can I take your drink order?" I looked up and there was Zoey.

I knew she had gotten a job, but I had no idea it was here. I hoped that she would maintain and keep the shit professional because if she didn't. Well, let's just say I would get full custody of our daughter.

"Hey, I didn't know you worked here," I said.

"Yea, I just started a few days ago. I certainly didn't expect to see you and your um, baby mama here," she said, eyeing Malaysia.

"You want to keep your job, right? Then I suggest you either serve us as you would anybody else in here or today will be your last day," I threatened.

"What can I get you to drink?"

"I'll have a coke and get Malaysia a glass of milk," I said, smiling at Malaysia.

"Oh wow! You let your man order for you. You don't know how to order your own drink?" Zoey asked Malaysia.

"I can order my own drink just fine, but my man knows what I like. So can you just bring us our drinks please?" Malaysia said with a smirk on her face.

"Be right back," Zoey said.

"Oh, and don't think about doing anything to our drinks or food either. Otherwise you'll have to answer to me," I told Zoey.

"Yea I know," she said as she rolled her eyes.

I honestly did not know that this girl worked here and from the look on Malaysia's face, I could tell she was uncomfortable. But I was not gonna let this chick run us out of this spot that I loved.

"You wanna leave?" I asked her.

"No, because I know you ain't no runner and neither am I."

"That's my girl," I said. "So, what do you think about Zay and Lexus being engaged?"

"Well, they do have that precious baby, so the two of them getting engaged was inevitable, I guess," she said.

"We're about to have a baby too. Do you think us getting engaged is inevitable?" I asked.

"Our situation is different from theirs."

"How so?" I asked.

Zoey came and brought our drinks and asked, "Are you ready to order?"

"Yes, I'll have the shrimp marinara please," Malaysia said.

"And I'll have the shrimp oreganata," I said and we handed her our menus.

"I guess you really can order your own food," Zoey said to Malaysia.

"Yea, not everyone is as slow as you, Zoey," Malaysia responded.

"Go get our damn food and remember what I said earlier," I jumped in before she could respond.

She hurried off and I could tell that she was mad, but I didn't give a shit. She was the worse baby mama I could have, especially with her mom involved.

"So, how is Lexus and Zay's relationship different from ours?" I asked again.

"Well for one, Lexus and Zay seem to be in love. Whereas, you haven't told me once that you love me. And second, Zay doesn't have to deal with your other baby mama drama. So, you see our situations are very different," she said.

"Do you want to get married, Malaysia?" I asked.

"What do you mean, to you or just in general?" She asked as she perched her chin on top of her hands as she stared at me.

"In general," I clarified.

"Well, every girl dreams of getting married one day. Of course, I hope to become someone's wife somewhere down the line," she said.

"Eventually, it'll happen for you."

"You sound like you got the inside scoop or something," she said.

"Nah, just confident that eventually you'll get everything you want."

"I hope so," she said.

Zoey returned with some bread in a basket and our plates of food. She placed mine in front of me then Malaysia's in front of her.

"Can I get you anything else?" she asked.

"Nah, we good," I said.

She turned and sashayed away from our table.

"What happened between you and Zoey?" Malaysia asked.

"She was just a fuck buddy that got pregnant. I already had an old lady, but Zoey offered me the pussy, so I took it. When she told me she was pregnant, no one was more surprised than me. At first, I wanted her to have an abortion because I didn't want Alize to find out, but she wouldn't do it.

After I saw my baby on the monitor for the first time, I was glad she didn't have an abortion. Zoey thought that when Alize found out, she would leave me, but she didn't. Alize stood by me through all of Zoey's bullshit," I said.

That was the truth. When Alize found out about Zoey, of course, she was upset. But she never left me. Zoey kept trying to do things to break us up, but Alize still stood by me. Had I not found her in my dad's office under his desk, I would have probably married her by now.

I know what my mom and Roz said, but I still went with my first mind. My first mind told me that she was sucking my dad's dick, so that was what I was going to believe. I refused to believe I killed my girl and my dad for nothing, so I was gonna stick with my first mind.

"Wow! Alize was really someone special. So, have you thought of hooking up with Zoey for more than just pussy? I mean, y'all do have a baby together. Have you ever thought about y'all becoming a family?" she asked.

"Hell no! Some chicks are meant to just be fucked, ya know? Other chicks are meant to be loved and taken care of," I said, smiling.

"Which category do I fit in?" she asked.

"You still here, so you should already know the answer to that question already."

I checked my watch and it was almost 8:45 PM. I polished off the rest of my food and asked Malaysia, "Are you ready?"

"Yea, I'm stuffed and a little sleepy," she said as she let out a yawn.

I raised my hand to signal Zoey to our table. She nodded her head, letting me know she was on her way. She was serving another table, so I waited for her to bring her ass over here. She finally brought herself to our table.

"Can I help you?" she asked with an attitude.

"We need our check," I said.

"I'll be right back," she said.

She walked away from the table and came back a couple of minutes later.

"Here you go. I hope you enjoyed your food," she said, smiling like a Cheshire cat.

"We did, thank you. I'm coming to get my daughter tomorrow, so have her ready," I said.

"You ain't taking my daughter around your booty girl," she said.

"She's not a booty girl. She's my fiancée," I said, knowing that I would get a rise out of her.

Almost immediately, you could see her facial expression change. Before she looked like she was enjoying herself trying to get under our skin. But now, she looked like she wanted to spit on us or slap the shit out of us for sure. I felt some satisfaction knowing that I had pissed her off. Of course, I was lying about Malaysia being my fiancée and her face almost reflected it, but she played along once she noticed how angry Zoey was.

"Stop lying. She don't even have no ring," Zoey said.

"Not yet, but she'll have one soon. So, you see, it doesn't do any good to keep Princess away from her because she's going to be her stepmother and our children are going to be siblings," I smiled as I stood up.

"I don't care if she's going to be my child's stepmother, I don't want her around my baby," Zoey said.

"You might as well get used to it because she's my daughter too and if you fuck with me, I will fuck with you," I said.

"Whatever! I don't want her around my baby," she said through clenched teeth.

"If it will make you feel better, I will treat your daughter just as I will treat my son," Malaysia smiled as she rubbed her protruding belly.

"No, that doesn't make me feel better, bitch!" Zoey said.

"Oooohhhh, I got your bitch!" Malaysia said, still smiling.

"I'll come by to pick up my daughter around one o'clock tomorrow afternoon and you better have her ready," I said as I grabbed Malaysia's hand and we walked out of the restaurant. The last thing I saw was Zoey fuming and cussing. She looked like her top was gonna be blown off her head at any moment. On the ride home, I got the text message I had been waiting for. The text was simple, yet satisfying. All it read was, 'Done'. That was all I wanted to see as I relaxed in my seat and enjoyed the rest of the ride. I knew this news would not be great for everyone, but it was the best news for me.

CHAPTER TWELVE

Malaysia

I must admit that messing with Zoey was fun. I was shocked when Princeton referred to me as his fiancée. I mean, sure we were talking about marriage, but he hadn't asked me to marry him, so why would he tell Zoey that. I cared a lot much about him, but he had to change some of his ways.

We couldn't be together if he continued to act a fool like he had been and we damn sure couldn't get married. I was only 18 and while he was 22, I still wanted to be with him. He would want to act right because if he didn't, I was gonna leave him and go right back to my mom's house. I didn't need to put up with all his bullshit.

"That was funny," he said.

"Yea, did you see the look on her face?" I asked.

"Hell yea. She looked like she was ready to beat the shit out of us."

"She sure did," I said as we burst into laughter.

He unlocked the doors and even walked me to my side of the car. He leaned me against the car and kissed me slow and sensual. When he first began to kiss me, I suspected he was doing it because he figured Zoey was watching. But the kiss was too heated for him to care about who was watching. When we parted lips, he kissed the tip of my nose and said, "Let's go home."

He opened the door for me, and I slid my thick body into the smooth leather seats. He closed the door then ran to the driver's side and got in. He leaned over, touched my stomach, and said, "You know, maybe we should get married."

I didn't know what his reason for saying that was, but I chose not to respond. He looked over at me and asked, "Did you hear what I just said?"

"Yea, I heard you," I said.

"So, what do you think about that?"

"I don't really know. I don't want you to marry me because I'm having your baby, Princeton. I mean, we've been together for almost nine months and you haven't even told me that you love me. I know any other woman would jump at the chance to marry you for your money, but I want to marry for love. If you don't love me, then we can't get married. I want a relationship like your mom and dad had. I won't settle for anything less for our son. He deserves to be in a happy family with two parents who love each other," I said.

I loved Princeton in my own way. I mean, if I had to speak the truth right now, I would say that I love Anthony too. I loved them both, but my heart was with Zay. I would stop messing with both of them if Zay said he wanted me. I didn't know what he saw in Lexus that he didn't see in me. I was a good woman and he enjoyed being inside me that night, I knew he did. If it killed me, I was going to get him back.

"Who said I didn't love you?" Princeton asked.

"You never said you did," I countered.

His phone began to ring, and he looked at the screen then picked up.

"Hey mom," he said.

There was silence and then he said, "Yea, she's right here. Do you need to speak to her?"

More silence and then he said, "We're on our way."

He ended the call and I asked, "What was that all about? It's late and I'm tired. I just want to go home and climb in the bed."

"My mom said we need to come over because the police are at your mom's house," he said.

"What are they doing at my mom's house?" I asked, pulling out my phone and dialing her number.

The phone rang six times before it went to voicemail. I hung up and repeated the action at least five more times with the same outcome. Why wasn't my mom answering her phone? What happened to her and why were the police there?

"Princeton hurry up! My mom isn't answering her phone. Something must be wrong!" I said.

"I'm going as fast as I can. You know I'm riding dirty, so I can't get caught speeding unless you want me to go to jail."

I sat back and just let him drive as I said a prayer for my mom that my mom was alright. I had never prayed so hard in my life, not even when those thugs were shooting at me. My mom was all I had, and she was the sweetest person. I suddenly wished I had stayed home with her when she asked me to. If I had done that, maybe none of this would be happening. As soon as we turned down the street, it was flooded with police and there was an ambulance present also.

Princeton pulled up as close as he could get. I didn't even wait for him to come to a complete stop before I jumped out and began running towards my mom's house. I was holding my belly as I ran. I tried to go inside the house but was stopped by the police.

"Sorry ma'am, but you can't go in there," he said.

"I live here, so please let me through," I begged.

"Hold up one minute. Don't move."

The officer turned around and went to talk to another officer in a white shirt. I slid under the yellow tape and ran up the steps to the entrance. When I walked in, I screamed because the place was a mess and there was blood everywhere. I looked around until I saw the sheet covering the body on the floor near the kitchen and dining room area.

This time my knees gave way right before I passed out.

*****

I didn't know what happened, but when I opened my eyes, I was in the back of an ambulance with Princeton and Ms. Yvonne sitting beside me.

"What am I doing in here? Where am I?" I asked, confused about my surroundings.

"You passed out, baby," Princeton said. Ms. Yvonne just sat there with tears in her eyes.

"Ms. Yvonne, what happened? Why are you crying?" I asked. I couldn't remember anything that happened before I ended up here. I was just so confused.

"Sweetheart, I hate to be the one to break the news to you," Ms. Yvonne said as tears flowed freely from her eyes.

"Break what news to me? What's going on? Is something wrong with the baby?" I asked as I reached for my swollen belly. My baby was moving around, so I knew that wasn't it. I looked from Princeton to his mom for answers. They both looked sad, but no one responded to me. "Princeton, what's going on? Why is your mom crying?"

Ms. Yvonne grabbed my hand and said, "I'm so sorry, Malaysia, but your mom is dead."

"What?! No, my mom isn't dead. I was just with her not that long ago," I said. "You're kidding, right?" I asked. I looked at Princeton, hoping that he would tell me that it was a big joke. He couldn't even look at me. "Please, tell me this isn't true." The pain I felt in my chest almost knocked me out. It was like a burning sensation as tears flooded my eyes.

"Ma'am, I'm going to need you to calm down for your baby's sake. If your blood pressure keeps spiking like this, we'll have to admit you. I need you to calm down or you'll go into premature labor. I know that isn't what you want," the emergency tech said. I didn't even know that he was in here. The ambulance wasn't moving either, so they needed to let me the fuck up outta here.

I reached for the oxygen mask that was on my face and attempted to remove it. "You need to leave that on for a little while. We may have to take you to the hospital," the paramedic stated.

"Okay, I'll try to calm down. Ms. Yvonne, please tell me that you weren't serious about my mom being dead. Please tell me that she's not dead," I begged with tears in my eyes. I just wanted someone to pinch me and wake me up from this bad dream I was having.

"I'm afraid I can't tell you that, hun. I wish I could, but…" she said with sad eyes.

"How? When? What happened? I was just with her a few hours ago," I said.

"We don't have any specifics yet, but it looks like somebody broke in and shot her. They think it was a robbery or something. That was all the information that I could get out of the police," Ms. Yvonne said.

"I'm so sorry, baby," Princeton said as he knelt beside me and held me while I cried.

I broke down and began to cry and bawl like a big baby. How could my mom be dead when I was just with her less than eight hours ago? I heard the blood pressure monitor beeping out of control and tried my best to calm down, but how could I? I just found out that my mom was dead. That meant that I'd never see her again.

That meant she'd never hold me again. That meant that she'd never be able to tell me she loved me again. That also meant that when I saw her earlier was the last time I'd ever see her alive again, and I didn't even get to tell her that I loved her.

"Baby, please calm down. Prince needs to stay inside just a little bit longer," Princeton said.

"Ma'am, I really need you to calm down or we'll have no choice but to bring you to the hospital. I can't afford to let you keep going like this, it's too dangerous for your baby. Your husband told me that you are due in six weeks, so please calm down," the EMT said.

"I'm trying, but it's hard. I loved my mom and she was all I had. Now I have no one," I cried.

"That's not true, Malaysia. You still have us, honey," Ms. Yvonne said.

My blood pressure continued to spike and the EMT said, "We're going to have to bring her in."

"Let me out, so I can follow y'all in my car. Mom, can you ride with Malaysia to the hospital please?" Princeton asked.

"Of course," Ms. Yvonne said.

Princeton leaned and kissed me on the lips before exiting the vehicle. The paramedic closed the door and prepared to put an IV in my hand.

"What are you doing?" I asked him.

"I need to inject this IV in your hand and start you on some hydralazine to help bring down your blood pressure. If I don't, then your baby will definitely come today and I don't want to chance it," he said.

After he injected the medication, I could feel my body begin to relax. I couldn't believe my mom was dead. I needed Princeton to find out who did this because I wanted them dead. When we arrived at the hospital, I was rushed to the emergency room while Ms. Yvonne was told to wait in the waiting room.

"Hello Miss Hughes, I'm Dr. Bradford and I'm the emergency room doctor on duty. We have put in a call to Dr. Tucker to let him know that you are here. Your blood pressure has descended since you were administered the hydralazine, but you aren't out of the woods yet. We'll be admitting you to the hospital overnight, so we can continue to monitor your blood pressure. If your blood pressure continues to spike, we'll have to do an emergency C-section, so we need you to remain calm," he said.

"I want my blood pressure to remain normal, but I received news that my mother was killed a little while ago. This really isn't how I intended to spend my evening," I said as tears began to flow again.

"I'm sorry to hear about your mother. But I must stress to you how important it is for you to keep your blood pressure down. If you go into premature labor, your baby will be sent to the prenatal intensive care unit because it's too early for you to deliver. According to the paperwork, you still have a little over a month before your due date. I just need you to calm down. Do you understand?" he asked.

"I understand," I said.

That was like telling me I couldn't grieve for my mom because my blood pressure would spike and endanger my baby. That was definitely the last thing I wanted to happen. With my mom gone, my baby was all I had left in the whole world.

"Good, because I would hate for you to go into premature labor," the doctor said.

All I could do was nod my head in understanding. I was so hurt, but I couldn't express my pain because I was pregnant. Who would break into my mom's house? All the years we had lived there, not once did anyone ever break in our home. My poor mom must have been scared to death. I couldn't even imagine what her last few moments were like.

"Is there someone that came with you?" he asked.

"My mother-in-law is in the waiting room."

"Would you like me to go get her for you?" Dr. Bradford asked.

I would much rather you get Zay and bring him down here, is what I said in my mind, but out loud I said, "Yes please."

"I'll be right back," he said.

I just lay back in the bed with my eyes closed, trying to think of good thoughts during this horrible tragedy. I thought back to the good times my mom and I used to share. I thought about how excited she was when I told her she was going to be a grandmother. Her eyes lit up like the sparklers for the fourth of July.

The doctor returned with Ms. Yvonne, who immediately sat next to me and held my hand.

"Try to keep her calm, ma'am. The life of her baby remains at risk as long as her blood pressure remains elevated," Dr. Bradford said.

"I will do my best, doctor. Thank you," Ms. Yvonne said. The doctor nodded his head and left the room.

"How are you feeling, hun?" Ms. Yvonne asked.

"I keep thinking that this has to be some kind of joke, Ms. Yvonne. I mean, I was with my mom earlier and now she's gone. Who would do this?" I asked.

"Who knows? People often do selfish things like that. Your mom was such a good woman. I'm going to miss our small talks about our children," she said.

"Where's Princeton?" I asked.

"He's on his way," she answered.

"This just seems so unreal."

"I contacted Lexus and Zay to let them know we are here," Ms. Yvonne said.

The moment I heard Zay's name, I perked up just a little. I was still hurt because my mom was dead but hearing that Zay knew about the situation gave me hope that this may have happened for a reason.

"What did they say?" I asked.

"Lexus said to let them know when you would be admitted into a room."

"What did Zay say about it?"

"I didn't speak to Zay, only to Lexus. But Princeton should be here soon," she said.

I wasn't worried about Princeton or his whereabouts right now. I just wanted Zay to come down here and see how I was doing. If he did, then it would mean that he cared about me more than he was willing to admit.

"She's in here," I heard a nurse say to someone outside my room.

I prayed that Zay would be the one to walk through that door. As I held my breath and waited to see who would walk in, my nerves got the best of me and the monitor began to beep wildly. Ms. Yvonne jumped up and asked, "Are you okay? Do you need me to call the doctor?"

"No ma'am, I'm fine," I said as I took deep breaths while rubbing my belly.

The door opened, and my heart sank when it was Princeton that walked in.

"How are you feeling?" he asked as he came to my bedside.

"I'm okay," I responded.

"The doctor said they would be moving you into your own room soon," he said.

"Yea, that's what they just told her. She needs to keep calm for the sake of the baby. The doctor said if her blood pressure keeps elevating that she could go into premature labor," Ms. Yvonne explained.

"Baby, you have to stay calm, okay? Our baby needs to bake in your oven for a few more weeks," Princeton said as he rubbed my stomach gently.

"I'm trying, but it's just hard," I said as tears began to slide down my face.

"I'm here for you, baby. You can just lean on me," Princeton said as he sat on the bed beside me and held me while I cried.

"We're here for you, Malaysia. If you're going to be with my son, you're family anyway," Ms. Yvonne said as she tried to force a smile, probably for my benefit.

"Thank you. Thank you so much," I said as I continued to cry while leaning against Princeton.

What was I going to do without my mom? As nice as it was to feel like I belonged to Princeton's family, it wasn't the same without my mom. I was having a baby in a few weeks, so I needed my mom to be here with me. I needed her guidance because I didn't know anything about being a mother. What if I failed my baby? I just didn't know what I was going to do without her.

I got moved to a private room an hour later and let's just say, it helped to comfort me a little bit. Knowing that I was on the same floor as Zay had my heart pumping, but my blood pressure remained steady. I didn't want to go into premature labor, but my nerves were bad because I knew that Zay was right down the hall. I still didn't know what I would do now that my mom was gone; she was literally my everything. Ms. Yvonne left a little while later to go see her granddaughter.

"You hungry? They said that you could eat," Princeton said.

"I am, but I don't know if I can eat anything right now."

"You have to eat because when you don't eat, our baby doesn't eat. So, what do you want?" he asked.

"Maybe a chicken sandwich from Wendy's," I said.

"Cool, I'll be back in a few minutes. Try and stay calm while I'm gone, okay?" he asked as he leaned in for a kiss.

"I will," I said.

A few minutes after he left, there was a knock on the door. I wondered who it could be since I wasn't expecting anyone, but the door slowly pushed open and in walked Anthony.

"What are you doing here, Anthony?" I asked. This was beginning to feel like Deja vu.

"I came for you, baby. I heard about your mom, so I went over to your house, only to see you being taken away by ambulance. I was so worried about you. Are you okay?" He asked as he held my hand and rubbed my belly. Almost immediately, our baby began to tumble all around in my stomach.

"I can't believe they killed my mom. Like she's really gone, and I'm never going to see her again. Anthony, why did this happen?" I asked as he held me close while stroking my hair.

"I don't know, baby, but I'll find out who did it for you. I promise," he said as he kissed my forehead.

"Anthony, you have to go. Princeton will be back here any minute and you can't be here when he gets back," I said.

"Why can't he know that I'm here? I'm tired of getting put out behind that no-good nigga. I love you and I wanna be here for you," he said.

"I just don't need you two going at it like last time. I'm in here because my blood pressure has been sky high and it's bad for the baby. They said if my blood pressure continues to rise, I'll go into premature labor. Is that what you want? For me to have my baby now when I still have six weeks left to go?" I asked.

"No, of course I don't want that. I love you and our baby, so I don't want anything to happen to either of you. I'll leave, but know that I'm thinking about you," he said.

"Thank you," I said as he kissed me softly on the lips.

He walked out, so I turned on the television and found the local news channel. I wanted to see if they would mention my mom and what happened to her. Just as I suspected, they did mention the story, so I turned the volume up.

"This is Mark Jansen reporting for News 12 Brooklyn, coming to you live outside of this brownstone where police were called here earlier this evening after hearing gunshots. Upon entry into the home, the police found a woman shot to death inside the home. The front door appeared to have been kicked in. The woman, who has been identified as Louise Hughes was inside during the invasion. The woman sustained multiple gunshot wounds to the chest, stomach and neck. It is unclear what the motive was behind the attack and the case is under investigation. Police ask that anyone who has information regarding this murder to please come forward. Again, this is Mark Jensen reporting for News 12 Brooklyn," said the reporter as he signed off.

I immediately broke into a fresh set of tears after hearing that. I was crying so hard I didn't even realize anyone was in the room with me until I felt his arms around me and smelled his hypnotizing scent. I looked up and sure as my name was Malaysia, there was Zay holding me as I cried. I held onto him tight and cried into his shirt.

"I'm sorry to hear about your mom," he said.

I didn't even answer because I didn't want to ruin the moment. I just held onto him and continued to cry as he stroked my hair. He eventually sat next to me on the bed and I took advantage of that moment. It felt so good to have his arms around me right now. I hadn't felt like this with anyone else and didn't know why I felt this strong attraction to Zay. I mean, it was only one night, and he had been ignoring me ever since.

"Is there anyone I can call for you?" he asked.

I shook my head no and said, "There's no one to call anymore. My mom was all I had and now she's gone."

"I'm sorry, but you know that we'll be here for you. I have to go back to Lexus' room. I just wanted to come and check on you and let you know that we're here for you if you need us," he said.

"I do need you, Zay. I've always needed you. Please don't leave me again!" I cried.

I know I was wrong for doing that. Here he was, checking on me while his fiancée was down the hall after just giving birth and here I was acting like a slut. But I couldn't help it. I needed him.

"I have to go," he said, trying to pull himself up from the bed.

I continued to hold onto him until I finally pressed my lips against his. I felt his resistance at first and then it felt like he was kissing me back. He pushed me back gently and said, "You have to stop this, Malaysia. I'm trying to offer you support, but that's it. I'm engaged to Lexus. We just had a baby, for God's sake! She's the one I love and she's the one I'm going to marry. Any fantasies that you have concerning us has got to stop. We'll never be together and if you continue this shit, I'll distance myself from you for good. Take care."

"Zay, don't leave me! Please Zay!" I cried at his back as he just walked out of the room.

"Aaaaarrrrrrggggggghhhhh!" I screamed and threw the plastic cup at the door. How could he just walk out on me during my time of need? I needed him more than ever and he just walked out on me.

I continued to cry like I had just found out my mom had died. Princeton walked in the room five minutes later and ran to my side to hold me. I allowed him to hold me as I cried while he soothed and tried to comfort me.

"Baby, it's gonna be alright. I love you and I'm here for you," he said.

What the fuck did he just say? Did this nigga just say he loved me? I had been waiting for him to give me a sign that he cared for me as more than just a booty call or baby mama. Now that he had finally said that he loved me, I wasn't sure how I felt. Why did he have to say it right after Zay just left here? Did he see Zay leave my room or something?

"What did you say?" I asked.

"Ummm, that it's gonna be alright," he said with a smile.

"You know darn well that's not what I'm talking about."

"I said I love you, Malaysia Janelle Hughes," he repeated.

"Why now? I've been waiting for you to say that for the last four months. Why would you pick today of all days to say it?"

"Because I think you should know that I'm going to be here for you. Now that your mom is gone, you can move in with me and we can turn the guest room into a nursery for Prince. We can be a family now," he said.

"But I don't want to move into Alize's house," I said.

I could see his face change and I knew I had said the wrong thing. I braced myself for what was to come.

"That is my house, not Alize's house. I don't understand why you won't move in when you are there most of the time anyway," he said.

"I just don't feel comfortable moving in the house you once shared with her," I said.

"Okay, I get that."

What? Is that it? No blow up. No argument. Just I get that. I looked at him and wondered if he was feeling okay, but I didn't push it.

"So, what do you get, Princeton?" I asked.

"You want a place of your own, like our own place. I get that," he said.

"Thanks."

"For what?"

"For not arguing with me about it," I said.

"Well, I don't want your blood pressure to rise up again and I can understand how you feel about it. I love you and I want to protect you," he said.

"Thank you, baby," I said as I gave him a kiss. "Now, where's my food? Because I'm starving."

CHAPTER THIRTEEN

Zay

I couldn't believe that Malaysia came on to me when I was trying to comfort her. I knew how close her, and her mom was, so I told Lexus I would go check on her and offer her my condolences. All I was trying to do was be a good friend to her and she had the nerve to make a move on me. I didn't want to upset Lexus since it was her idea for me to go to Malaysia's room, but I had to tell her. I wasn't going to keep this a secret from her.

I looked at my watch and it read 10:45 p.m. I just knew that Lexus would be asleep since Ms. Yvonne had probably gone home. But when I walked into the hospital room, Lexus was wide awake sitting in bed holding Za'Nya.

"Hey," I said.

"Hey yourself," she said with a smile.

"I thought you'd be asleep."

"Well, I just fed Za'Nya. But as tired as I am, I wanted to wait for you to get back, so I could ask how your visit with Malaysia went. How's she doing?" she asked, looking concerned.

"She's really heartbroken. I feel really bad for her. I asked if there was someone I could call for her, but she said she has no one else," I said.

"She doesn't. She doesn't know her dad and her mom was an only child so she really is all alone. She and her mom moved here several years ago, and we've been friends ever since. I just feel bad for her," she said.

This was going to make what I had to say to her even more difficult. Since she was Malaysia's only friend, I felt bad about coming in between them when they were just beginning to salvage their friendship. But, if Malaysia had ill intentions about being Lexus' friend, Lexus deserved to know. I just wasn't sure how I would tell her that Malaysia made a pass at me? I felt bad that they were trying to rebuild their friendship, but Malaysia had definitely crossed the line. I really didn't know what to do because I had conflicting feelings about the situation.

On one hand, I didn't want to keep this a secret from Lexus. But on the other hand, how could I tell her and destroy a friendship that was already treading on thin ice? I decided to let them work on their friendship since Malaysia didn't have any family to help her through this difficult time.

I took Za'Nya from Lexus and changed her diaper. I wrapped her up in her little blanket and placed her in the hospital bassinette. I kissed Lexus good night and prepared to get comfortable on the hospital sofa bed. I hoped they would discharge my girls tomorrow because I didn't know how much more of this shit I could take.

*****

The next morning, I woke up and headed to the office to check on a shipment. I didn't want to disturb Lexus, so I left her a note near her bed. When I arrived at the building, even though it was only six o'clock in the morning, my crew was bustling and moving, grinding was all it was about. I loved to see this type of activity so early in the morning because hustlers never slept. When a hustler slept, he took the chance that he could be missing out on something big. I wasn't going to be that hustler.

"Hey man, did you hear the news?" Chico asked me.

"What news?" I asked.

"Word on the street has it that it was the Nigerians that shot up the truck that Malaysia was in," he said.

"Whoa! So, they found out it was Princeton who put out the hit on Taurus. Wow!" I said.

"Yea, that just goes to show that what is done in the dark always comes to light," Chance said.

"You got that right," I affirmed. "So, are we on for receiving that shipment tonight?"

"Fa sho," Chico said.

"Okay then, let me get back to the hospital because I think my girls are coming home today," I said.

"Yea, how is your little princess and the queen?" Chance asked.

"They're great! She couldn't be a more perfect baby and Lexus took that childbirth experience like a champ."

"So, y'all gonna make another one?" Chico asked.

"Naw, not for a little while anyway. I mean, our little one is just two days old," I said as we laughed.

"Well, we will hit you up later then. Go check on your girls because I know the queen doesn't like to wait," Chico said as we laughed again.

"You got that right," I said.

I dapped it up with my boys then shot out to go scoop up my girls. I walked out to my truck and got in. I was about to back out when Princeton pulled up behind me. I should have known it wouldn't be long before me and this nigga squared off again. I took my piece out of my waistband and placed it in the secret compartment in my truck. I was going to fight his ass, not shoot him; at least not yet. He wasn't going to catch me off guard this time; nah, this time I was ready.

"What you doing here, man?" I asked.

"You should've known you would be seeing me again, especially after I saw you playing kissy face with my sister yesterday," he said.

"Look man, I don't know what your problem is. It's like you don't want to see your sister happy. I mean, we just had a baby and yet here you are acting all macho and trying to throw your weight around."

"I told you from day one to stay away from my sister. All I asked was that you listen and take heed to my warnings," he said.

"You know what? Your sister is a grown ass woman and she's able to make her own decisions. I'm a grown ass man and I don't take orders from you. Besides, what's done is done. We're getting married and we're going to be a family...PERIOD! Now, if you wanna fight, we can do that shit because I'm tired of your bullshit. Everyone in the family is happy for us, except yo ass. I don't have time for all this shit you spitting out right now. So, what you wanna do?" I asked.

I was more than ready to beat this nigga's ass. I had enough of him and all that "you didn't do as I said" shit. He stepped closer to me and took a swing at me, but I was waiting for his punk ass to do that shit, so I ducked. I came back and hit him with a two-piece combo and the fight was on. We began punching each other until he lost his footing and fell back. I guess we were making a lot of noise and commotion because next thing I knew, my team had run outside to cheer me on.

I didn't want to brag, but I was really kicking that nigga's ass. I had to stop myself because he looked like he was about to be unconscious. I stood up and Chico brushed the dust off my back. I reached my hand out to help Princeton up, but he slapped it away.

"C'mon man, let's squash this shit and just be happy. Aren't you tired of fighting something you ain't got no control over?" I asked him.

"Fuck you!" he said as he stood up, brushed himself off, and jumped in his car. He backed out and sped off.

"Yo, you aight, man?" Chance asked.

"Yea, I'm good," I said. "That nigga ain't did shit to me."

"What the fuck was that about?" Chico asked.

"You know that nigga really hates seeing me with his sister. I mean, we live together, we're engaged, and we just welcomed a beautiful baby girl into the world. What will it take for his ass to just accept the fact that me and Lexus are together?" I asked.

"Some people just don't get it. That nigga is definitely buggin'," Chance said.

"I'm gonna head out. I need to go home and change before I go pick up Lexus and Za'Nya from the hospital. I'ma get up with y'all later," I said as I got in my truck and headed home.

I didn't want to fight Princeton because I felt that we were fighting for nothing. He was fighting me because I was with Lexus, but that's something he couldn't change. He would never be able to break us up, so I didn't understand why he couldn't just get with it. I mean, he was with Malaysia and no one was trying to break them up.

My phone rang when I was five minutes away from the house.

"Hello," I said.

"Hey baby, the doctor will be discharging me and Za'Nya in about an hour. Can you come pick us up?" Lexus asked.

"Fa sho. I'm on my way."

"Okay, see you when you get here," she said, and we ended the call.

I made it home and parked in the garage. I went inside, so I could take a shower and get dressed before heading back to the hospital. I accessed the wounds from the fight with Princeton, which weren't too bad. I had a bruised cheek, a busted lip, and a small cut under my left eye. I also had a couple of scrapes from when we were fighting on the ground, but it wasn't anything I couldn't handle.

I showered, got dressed, then headed out to go pick up my girls. I was so excited to have them home. I jumped in the car and headed over to the hospital to pick them up. When I arrived at the hospital, I pressed the UP button on the elevator and waited for it to stop.

When I got to the room, imagine how surprised I was to see Malaysia holding our baby. I swear, that girl had some loose screws or something. She definitely had a lot of nerve being here after the shit she pulled yesterday.

"Hey babe," Lexus said.

"Hey. Hey Malaysia," I said.

"Hey Zay. I just had to come and see your baby girl again. She's so adorable," she said.

"Yea, she is that," I said, moving closer to her to take our baby.

"Well, I know that my son will be just as precious as she is since they have the same bloodline. Lexus told me that she and the baby are being discharged today. That's great!" she said.

"Yea, I'm happy to be going home. I miss my bed," Lexus said with a smile.

"I know what you mean. I have been maintaining a low blood pressure, so I'm sure that the doctors will release me today also," Malaysia said.

"That's good," I said.

"Malaysia was telling me that she appreciated you stopping by the room yesterday," Lexus said.

"Yea, I reaaaalllyy appreciated it," Malaysia said.

"No problem," I said.

"Well, maybe when I'm released, we can chill at your new place," Malaysia said to Lexus.

"Maybe," Lexus responded. "Zay, what happened to your face? I'm just noticing those fresh cuts."

"Oh, it's nothing," I said.

She jumped off the bed she was sitting on and came to inspect the minor bruises from my fight with her brother. She touched my cheek where the bruise was and the one under my eye. "Who did you get in a fight with?"

"I bet it was Princeton," Malaysia said.

"Was it my brother you fought with?" Lexus asked.

"Yea, but it was nothing, like I said. He came by the office and was pissed because of our engagement, so I had to handle him. I don't think we'll be having that discussion again any time soon," I said.

"I just don't get why my brother can't see that we love each other and there's nothing he can do to break us up. I mean, even if you agreed to end it with me, I wouldn't let you. We have a baby now and we're a family. If he can't accept that, well, I feel sorry for him," Lexus said.

"C'mon, you know I'm never letting you go," I said as I leaned in for a kiss.

The look on Malaysia's face when I pulled away was one that showed nothing but disdain. I could tell that she was ready to snatch Lexus' hair and I had to wonder why she was so upset. I knew she wanted the two of us to get together, but that was never going to happen. I knew for a fact that I had made myself clear when I spoke to her yesterday.

"You guys look so happy," Malaysia said with a fake smile plastered on her face.

"We are blissfully happy," I said, just in case she had any other ideas.

"A little birdie told me that you were ready to go home," the doctor said as she walked in.

"You have no idea," Lexus said.

"Well, I got your discharge papers right here, along with that precious baby girl," she said.

"I'm going to give you these papers, which are instructions on how to care for yourself and your baby once you get home. I'd suggest that you not lift anything over ten pounds for the next three weeks. Also, get out of bed and walk at least three times a day, even if it's just in the house. No driving or operating any motor vehicle for the next two weeks. If you should start clotting, please don't hesitate to come in. And I don't think I should have to tell you to abstain from any sexual activity for the next six weeks, or at least until I give you the okay. I made an appointment for you in two weeks and for the baby in one week with Dr. Brody. Any questions?" she asked.

"No ma'am. I appreciate everything you did, and I'll see you in two weeks," Lexus said.

"Okay, if you will sign here and here, you'll be free to go," the doctor said.

Lexus signed the papers in the designated areas and the doctor handed her the copies, along with several packets of information and some freebies for Za'Nya. I put our precious cargo in her car seat and strapped her in. The nurse came with a wheelchair because it was standard procedure for the patient to be wheeled downstairs.

"Well, I guess I better head back to my room. Lexus, I'll talk to you later," Malaysia said.

"Yea, sure. I just want you to know that we're here for you. If you need help planning your mom's funeral, don't hesitate to call me. Okay?" Lexus asked as she gave Malaysia a hug. Malaysia looked at me and blew me a kiss, which had the nurse looking at me all crazy.

What was with this fucking girl, man? Now, the nurse was looking at me as if I was some kind of cheater. I knew how things must have looked to her. I mean, here I was with the woman who had just given birth to our daughter, yet this pregnant woman was blowing kisses at me while hugging my fiancée. I was sure she must have thought that I was some kind of scumbag.

As we rode in the elevator, I could feel the uncomfortable stares from the nurse. It was weird because I hadn't done anything wrong, but I was starting to feel like a big pile of shit.

CHAPTER FOURTEEN

Malaysia

Lexus was so blind and too damn trusting if you asked me. I wanted Zay and I knew that he could see it in my eyes. What I didn't understand was why he continued to play these games as if he wasn't interested. I knew he wanted me and if it was the last thing I did, I was gonna make sure he got me. I tried my best to get over him, especially since I was with Princeton, but I couldn't break this hold he had on me.

When I made the decision to go see Zay and Lexus' baby girl, I was really looking for him. But he wasn't there, so of course I had to play it off. I sat there staring at their gorgeous baby, wishing that she were mine. She had a little nose like her dad, and she was just so cute.

I didn't want to give her back to him, but the feel of his skin brushing against mine was well worth it. I wanted more than just our hands touching though. I wanted him to fuck me the way he did that first night with his big dick.

When he walked in and saw me holding his baby, I could tell that he was surprised to see me. I couldn't help but notice how pissed he was too. I half expected him to say something about our little visit yesterday, but I should've known better. I knew he wouldn't say anything about the kiss that we shared. My toes were still curling from that shit and my panties were still wet too.

I was anxious to get out of this hospital, so I could go fuck Princeton or Anthony. I was super horny, so horny I almost forgot that my mom was dead. The pain of losing her washed over me once again and I felt the need to break down and cry. I tried my best to hold it in until I got to my room, but as I walked Lexus and Zay out of their room, I felt tears burning my eyes.

I managed to make it to my room just in time to receive a visit from my doctor.

"I see you've been walking and getting around," Dr. Langley said.

"Yes, I had a friend who just delivered her baby, so I went to see her before she was discharged. So, are you going to release me today?" I asked.

"I'm a little hesitant to discharge you since your blood pressure is still on the borderline from time to time. But you seem to be doing really good today, so I'll let you go home. If you feel any kind of discomfort or you get any cramps, please don't hesitate to come back to the hospital," he said.

"I will," I promised.

"Okay, well give me a couple of hours and I'll be back to check on you. This will give you a chance to call someone to come pick you up," he said.

"I'm already here," said Anthony, shocking the shit out of both me and Dr. Langley.

"Oh, hello young man," the doctor turned to him and said.

"Wassup doc," Anthony said as he came to stand next to me.

I was sure Dr. Langley was confused because Princeton had been the only man here with me the whole time. Now, Anthony was here, rubbing my belly and looking every bit the proud papa. Dr. Langley must have thought I was a hoe.

"Well, I'll leave you two alone. I'll go fill out your discharge papers since your ride is here," the doctor said.

I was so embarrassed, and I knew my face reflected those emotions. I was in such a shock that I couldn't even move. All I could do was look at Anthony as the doctor walked out the room.

"Why are you here?" I asked, not bothering to show how angry I was.

"You heard the doc. I'm here to spring you from this place," he smiled.

"I'm not leaving with you Anthony. Princeton will be here to get me soon."

"What is wrong with you? All I want is to be here for you, especially now that your mom is gone. I want to be a father to our baby, why won't you let me? Is it because that nigga has money and you're some gold digger?" he asked, his voice mixed with pain and anger.

"I love him," I simply said.

"No, you don't. You love me," he said as he looked down at me with sad eyes.

"Not true. I love him," I repeated.

He leaned closer to me and pressed his lips to mine. I wanted to stop him, but my body reacted, and I found myself kissing him back. I wrapped my arms around his neck and inserted my tongue in his mouth as the kiss grew more passionate. I didn't stop him when he pulled me towards the bathroom and locked the door.

I was so fucking horny that I needed to feel him inside me. He had me leaned up against the sink as he inserted his dick in me from behind. I cried out as my body reacted by extracting my love potion onto his dick. He continued to slide his dick in and out of me and that made me feel so good.

I was looking at him in the mirror as he watched my face change from the intense pressure his dick was putting on my insides. Anthony and I had always been great in the bedroom. He knew exactly how to hit that spot that made me cry out; the way I was doing now.

I knew that what we were doing was wrong. This was absolutely not the time or the place with so many people having access to my room. But I couldn't stop Anthony from giving it to me if I wanted to and God knew me too well to know that I didn't want to.

"Yea, that's it. Hit it right there!" I cried then bit my lip as he drove his dick deeper into me.

He leaned back and sat on the toilet with his dick still inside me as I rode it reverse cowgirl style. Oh God, did that feel good. I was rotating my hips like a belly dancer, grinding onto him as my pussy swallowed his dick over and over again.

"Miss Hughes," the nurse said as she knocked on the bathroom door.

"Yessssss!" I cried.

"Miss Hughes are you alright?" she asked.

"Oh yes, I'm fine," I replied as I continued to ride Anthony's big dick. I wanted to get off and go see what the nurse wanted, but I couldn't. I really needed this dick and I wasn't stopping until I was done getting mine.

"Do you need me to get the doctor? You don't sound too good," she said.

"Oh God! I'll be out in a minute," I whispered.

"What was that, Miss Hughes?" she asked.

"I said I'll be out in a minute," I said a little louder as my body shook from the massive orgasm that I was having.

"Oh God! Oooooohhhhhh!" I cried as Anthony continued his assault on my pussy.

"I'm getting the doctor for you," the nurse said.

"Noooooooooo! Oh God! I promise I'm just fine." I tried to reassure her that I was okay, so she wouldn't go get Dr. Langley. The last thing I needed was for him to come through that door and find out that I was having sex in the bathroom.

I heard the door to my room close and I knew she went to get the doctor. Anthony grabbed my swollen breasts and thrust one last time into me before he released inside me. Oh my God! I really needed that.

I slowly stood up on my wobbly knees and walked over to the sink, splashing cold water on my face as Anthony raised his pants up. I slowly made my way out of the bathroom while he remained inside for a couple of minutes. I was sitting on the bed with my IV cart next to me when the nurse walked in with Dr. Langley.

"Are you alright, Miss Hughes?" the doctor asked.

"I am absolutely fine," I answered.

"Are you sure? You look a little flushed," he said.

"I'm fine. Did you come to discharge me?" I asked.

"Well Nurse Marie came and got me because she said that she didn't think you were feeling well and that you were locked in the bathroom. I wanted her to remove your IV," he said.

"I feel fine and I told her I didn't need you," I said, eyeing the nurse.

"You sounded like you were in pain, Miss Hughes. I wouldn't be doing my job if I didn't get Dr. Langley; just in case you were in any kind of distress," she said.

"Thank you, but had I been in any kind of distress, I would've pulled the little string next to the toilet," I said.

Anthony finally emerged from the bathroom guilt written all over his face. We smiled at each other and I thought the nurse and doctor figured out why I was locked in the bathroom as they exchanged a look of their own. The nurse began to remove the IV from my hand and patched up the hole with a bandage.

"Let me go get your paperwork," Dr. Langley said.

The nurse finished up, grabbed her things and walked out.

"Anthony, you have to go now. Princeton will be here soon, and I don't want a confrontation between the two of you," I said.

"After what just happened between us, you still want me to leave?" he asked, looking hurt and disappointed.

"I'm dealing with too much right now. I can't afford to be stressed out with you guys. Please just do this for me. Please," I begged.

He walked over to me and wrapped me in his arms. He lifted my chin with his forefinger and kissed me on the lips.

"I love you, Malaysia. I mean, I really love you, but I won't be a fool for love much longer," he said.

He touched the tip of my nose and then he was gone. I picked up my phone to call Princeton and let him know I was getting discharged, so he could come get me, but he didn't answer. I called again and got no answer. I tried two more times and then I just set the phone down because he wasn't answering my calls. Where could he be and why wasn't he answering me?

CHAPTER FIFTEEN

Princeton

I saw that Malaysia was calling me, but I was in the middle of something. Shit, I figured since she was in the hospital, she wasn't going anywhere anytime soon. After the fight with Zay, I somehow ended up at Zoey's place. I guess it was because her apartment was closer to Zay's office than my condo. I stopped over to get myself cleaned up before I went to pick up Malaysia from the hospital.

I knocked on Zoey's door several times before she finally answered. She opened the door and said, "Who the fuck knocking..."

She didn't finish her sentence when she saw me standing there with blood on my face.

"What the fuck happened to you?" she asked as she crossed her arms over her chest.

"Don't worry about it. Can I come in and clean myself up?" I asked.

"Yea, but why didn't you go to your own place?" she asked as I pushed her aside.

"Don't worry about that shit either," I said, heading to her bathroom.

"Where's my baby girl?" I asked.

"She spent the night with my mom because Deidre's kids are over there," she said.

Deidre was her sister and sometimes she went out of town on business and left her kids at their mom's house. I began washing my face and hands. A black eye was beginning to form, and I had a cut on my forehead. My lip was cut from me biting it when Zay punched it between my teeth. That nigga was gonna pay for this shit. When I came out of the bathroom I looked at Zoey for the first time and noticed the lil booty shorts she had on.

Those shorts were so short, her ass cheeks were playing peek-a-boo with me. I wasn't gonna lie because Zoey was one fine bitch. She had some big breasts, a fat ass, and a small waist, even after having our child.

"You finished?" she asked.

"Why? You trying to put me out?" I asked, moving close to her.

She backed up and said, "Hell yea! I'm trying to go back to sleep because I have to work tonight. You remember my job, right? The place you brought your lil heifer to."

"I remember," I said as I stood in front of her. I had her pinned against the wall.

"Move boy!" she said, trying to move pass me.

"Boy? I got ya boy."

"Nah, whatever you got, go give it to your other baby mama. I don't want it no mo," she said, pushing my chest in an effort to get me out the way.

"I wanna give it to you. How long has it been since we made love?" I asked as I dipped my head to nibble on her earlobe.

"Move Princeton, shit!" she said.

"Feel this dick and tell me you don't want it." I said as I rubbed her hand against my growing shaft.

"Move boy," she said, but I could tell I was getting to her.

I rubbed my hand on the front of her shorts, feeling on her pussy. I began to kiss her neck and a soft moan escaped her lips. I began to suck on her neck and that was it. Next thing I knew, her shorts were on the floor and my pants were wrapped around my ankles as I fucked her against the wall.

She screamed my name as I pounded viciously into her pussy. It had been a long time since she and I had fucked, but it was just like old times as soon as I felt her tight pussy clutch my dick. I moved her off the wall and picked her up and down, guiding her on my dick.

I slowly moved towards the bed, where I dropped her little 5'6" frame and took off my shirt. Her pussy was shaved in that Brazilian wax style and it was calling my name. I thrust my tongue inside her and fucked her with my tongue. She cried out as she gripped my curly hair and rode my tongue.

I continued to lick her until I could taste her juices, then I put both of her legs on my shoulders and plowed into her pussy again. Her perky breasts bounced up and down, making me work harder.

"Oh God! I'm fixin' to cum!" she cried.

"Cum on this dick! Cum all over this big dick!" I said as I continued to fuck her hard.

"Oh my! Fuck me, Princeton!" she said.

"Turn over," I said as I pulled out.

She quickly got on all fours. I got behind her and rammed my dick inside her, causing her to scream. I smacked her ass while I plunged into that pussy real good. I wanted her to feel every single inch of me as I wore her pussy out.

I grabbed her ponytail and continued to fuck her. I wanted my dick to leave its prints all over the inside of her pussy. It didn't matter if we were together or not, this was gonna always be my pussy.

"Whose pussy is this?" I asked.

"That's my pussy, muthafucka!" Was all I heard before someone hit me behind the head.

I was in a daze and butt naked as this dude was wailing punches on me left and right. I finally got myself together and started swinging back on his ass. I didn't know how I managed to do it, but I got my gun from my pants and began pistol whipping his ass. He wanted to fuck with me, then he was gonna see what the consequences was for fucking with a boss nigga like me.

"Princeton, stop! You're going to kill him!" I heard Zoey screaming.

I finally let up on the nigga, who was a bloody unconscious mess at my feet. I went in the bathroom and cleaned myself up again before returning to put my clothes on. Zoey was trying to wake the dude up, but she wasn't having any luck.

"Why the fuck you didn't tell me about that nigga? You gave that muthafucka a key to your place and was fucking me? You are a foul bitch, Zoey!" I yelled.

"Bitch?! You got a lot of damn nerve calling me a bitch when you got another woman pregnant!" she screamed.

"Yea, you a bitch!" I said.

"Get the fuck out my house, Princeton!" she yelled, getting up in my face. I mushed her fucking ass hard to the face, sending her flying across the floor.

"Fuck you bitch and yo bitch ass nigga! Y'all can both kiss my black ass!" I said before I walked out of the apartment. I heard her trying to wake that nigga up on my way out, but the way I just beat his ass, it was gonna take a miracle to get his ass up. I knew I didn't kill him, but he'd most likely be out of it all fucking day long.

I headed over to the hospital to check on Malaysia. I pulled out my phone to let her know that I was on my way and noticed that she had called over fifteen times. I hit the talk button on my phone and her phone started to ring.

"Where the hell are you?" she asked.

"I'm on my way, girl! You better chill the fuck out with all that attitude, yo!" I said.

"I got discharged 45 minutes ago and I'm just been sitting here waiting for yo ass, so don't tell me to chill the fuck out. You need hurry the fuck up!" she said and ended the call.

Man, what the fuck was up with the women in my life these days? All they wanted to do was back talk and shit. I was feeling some kind of way about Zoey and that nigga. The more I thought about it, the more I wanted to kill their asses.

I realized I had anger issues and I might need help maintaining and managing it, but I liked my way better. The gun was always a better solution than sitting in some quack's office, listening to them tell you that you needed to calm down or count to 20. Bitch! I got better things to do than sit in that office and count to 20. I could just count to five and blow those bitches to smithereens and finish with that.

*****

I arrived at the hospital 20 minutes later and went upstairs to find Malaysia pissed off.

"Can you take me to my house please?" she asked angrily.

"What? I thought you was coming home with me after what happened to your mom. I mean, do you really want to go home and see all those blood stains and shit? And besides, I don't think the police removed the crime scene tape yet, so you can't go in," I said.

In case y'all didn't guess it yet, I was the reason her mom was dead. The reason I had my men kill her mom was because I was tired of all her shit talking.

That woman had too much damn nerve and way too much time on her hands to be speaking to me like she did, but I bet she'd never speak to me like that again. And besides, if Malaysia had no place to go, then she'd have no choice but to stay with me, so I could keep an eye on her. I didn't want her to be traipsing all over the place, putting my little man in jeopardy. And if she still had something going on with that punk ass muthafuckin' Anthony, I would kill them both.

"I guess I have no choice but to go home with you then," she said, walking out of the room.

"Hey, why you acting like that?" I asked.

"This is not the time or the place to discuss this. We can talk about it in the car," she said.

We got in the elevator and all I could think of was this chick is really feeling herself right now.

She had to be to feel like she could talk to me like that and get away with it. Baby or no baby, I needed to let her know who was in charge because apparently, she was thinking a nigga had gotten soft or something.

We drove to my place in silence and when we arrived, she jumped out the truck and hurried to the front door. I unlocked it and she waddled her ass to the bathroom and turned on the shower.

"Aye, we need to talk," I said.

"We can talk later. I just want to hop in the shower because I'm tired of smelling like the hospital."

I grabbed her by her arm and said, "That wasn't a request."

She jerked her arm out of my grasp and sat down on the bed, arms across her chest.

"What the fuck is wrong with you, Malaysia?" I asked.

"Oh, I don't know. Maybe, it's the fact that I had to wait almost two hours for you to come get me. Maybe, it's the fact that I've been calling you all morning and you didn't bother to pick up once. Or maybe, MAYBE, it's the fact that you came to pick me up smelling like pussy!" she cried.

What? She could smell pussy on me. Nah, she was just fishing to see if I was fucking instead of being at the hospital with her.

"Maybe what you smelling is your own pussy. You sure can't be smelling no pussy on me," I said.

"Whatever Princeton. I believed you the other night when you said you loved me. When I found out about my mom getting killed, you were there for me, so I thought maybe you really did love me. But you don't. The only person you love is yourself," she said.

By this time, she was in tears and I wanted to comfort her and tell her that it wasn't true. I wanted to hold her and let her know that I did care about her, but the truth was she really was smelling pussy on me because I forgot to brush my teeth and wash my face after eating Zoey's pussy.

"That's not true. I do care about you and our baby," I said.

"Whatever. Can I go take my shower now? I really am exhausted," she said.

"Yea," I said.

I waited until she was taking her shower then grabbed my toothbrush and applied some toothpaste to it. I went in the other bathroom to brush my teeth and wash my face. I returned to the bathroom and stripped my clothes off.

I slid the glass door open to find Malaysia crying in the shower. I didn't want her to cry and if she was crying because of me, I certainly didn't want that either. I turned her around to face me and held her close to me.

At first, she resisted, but then she allowed me to hold her as she shed tears for her mom, I guess. My dick began to grow as I stood close to her naked body. I lifted her face to mine and kissed her. She kissed me back slow and timidly, as if she wasn't sure she wanted to kiss me. I thrusted my tongue in her mouth and it began to dance with hers.

She felt so soft in my arms and before long, we were making love in the shower. She called out my name as I hit that G-spot over and over again. I had this nut ready to bust since I was up in Zoey's pussy and I'd be damned if I let it go to waste.

I pumped in and out of her until I finally released my load. I gave her a kiss and said, "I'm sorry."

She just smiled and nodded her head. She began to lather herself up and I did the same. When we were finished, we dried each other off and headed to the bedroom. She got between the sheets, butt ass naked and I decided to lay with her.

"Are you gonna tell me what happened to you today?" she asked.

"Babe, I just apologized for my behavior. Can't we just squash that?" I asked.

"That's not what I'm talking about. What happened to your face?" she asked, touching my cuts and bruises.

"I got in a fight."

"With Zay, huh?"

"Yea, but how you figure that out?" I asked.

"I was visiting Lexus when he walked in with his own bruises. She asked him what happened, and he said y'all had gotten in a fight. What were y'all fighting about or do I even need to ask?"

"Same shit just a different day," I responded.

"Babe, why can't you just let it go? I mean they're engaged, living together and have a new baby. That man isn't going anywhere," she said.

"Oh, he'll go somewhere. I don't care if I have to knock him off the face of the earth my damn self."

"It isn't that serious."

"Enough about that. You hungry?" I asked, rubbing her belly. I spoke to her belly, "Hey lil man. I can't wait to meet you, son. I love you so much." I kissed her on her belly.

"You know how much things are going to change once he gets here?" she asked.

"What you mean by that?"

"I mean, we're going to be parents."

"In case you forgot, babe I'm already a parent," I said, laughing.

"Yea, I know, but I'm gonna be a mommy," she said.

"Yea. Are you excited?"

"Hell yea! I hope he looks just like you," she said.

"Yea, me too. I'm gonna go get us a pizza from Pizza Hut. You want some wings or something?" I asked.

"No, but make sure that pizza is large with some jalapenos. You know I love the peppers," she said.

"Yea, I know."

I gave her a kiss and got dressed. I grabbed my bills and keys, then headed for the door. I didn't know how long this shit would last, but I was gonna just roll with it and play it by ear.

CHAPTER SIXTEEN

Malaysia

Four days later...

Today was the day I would say my final goodbyes to my queen, my mom. I missed her so much and wondered who would be so cruel as to take her life. So far, the police had no suspects, and no one would come forward with any information. That was the one thing I hated about our neighborhood; if something happened, no one was willing to say shit about what they saw.

Princeton was nice enough to pay for my mom's funeral expenses. I didn't even know if my mom had a life insurance policy. Princeton had ordered her a beautiful soft pink coffin since that was her favorite color. The inside was lined with pink also and she had tons of flowers. The funeral home and church was packed. It made me smile to see how many people really cared about my mom.

When it was time to read the eulogy, I prayed that my legs would hold steady for me to see it through. I hated that I'd never see my mom again. I'd never hear her laugh again. I really missed my ladybug. Once I finished reading the eulogy, I cleared my throat and began speaking about my mom.

"My mom was one of the kindest people I knew. She was so excited when I told her that I was pregnant with her first grandchild. She worked hard to raise me by herself and I know she did a great job because I wouldn't be here today if it wasn't for her. It pains me that she won't be here to see her grandson make his entrance into the world.

That's the saddest part; that my mom won't be alive to see her grandchild. Mommy, I love you and I miss you so much. Please watch over me and Prince from heaven. Until we meet again, I'll just have our wonderful memories. Thank you all for coming to see my mommy off. I truly appreciate the support," I said.

The choir broke into one of my mom's favorite songs, Boys II Men & Mariah Carey's, *One Sweet Day,* as I was walking back to my seat.

Sorry I never told you

All I wanted to say

And now it's too late to hold you

'Cause you've flown away

So far away

Princeton held me as I cried while the choir continued to sing. The pastor did the closing prayer and then it was time to lay my mom to rest. I thanked God for Princeton because I couldn't have gotten through any of this without him. He had been a huge support to me since my mom passed away.

Once the funeral was over, all I wanted to do was go home and lie down. Princeton and I had made arrangements for a homegoing luncheon, just like the one they had for his dad, but I didn't want to go. I just couldn't take another minute of being around all those people. All I wanted was to go home, climb in bed, and go to sleep.

"You wanna go to the dinner?" he asked as we got in the limo.

"No, I just wanna go home," I said as I leaned my head against him.

"You want something to eat?" he asked.

"No."

"Babe, you have to eat because you're not eating for just you. Think of our son," he said.

"I'll fix a sandwich when I get home, but I just want to go home please," I said.

"Aight," he said as he held me close.

After a few minutes, he said, "It really was a beautiful service."

I just nodded my head. I didn't wanna talk or think about the funeral anymore. I had just watched my mom's casket get lowered into the ground and as much as I wanted to get that image out of my head, I knew it would be a long time before that happened. My mom was gone and there was nothing anyone could say or do to change that.

The limo driver dropped us off at the condo and Princeton gave him five hundred bucks for his time and service. I was just too damn drained to care about anything right now. I undressed and climbed into bed and I guess I fell asleep.

CHAPTER SEVENTEEN

Lexus

Three months later...

Our little girl was so cute, and she was growing like a little weed. She had the brightest eyes and the cutest lips. She had finally started sleeping through the night and I was so in love with her. Zay was the perfect daddy and I felt blessed to have him in our lives.

I heard that Malaysia had given birth to a beautiful baby boy they named Prince Clark six weeks ago. I was happy that she hadn't named him Princeton Jr. after my brother. I went to visit her when she was in the hospital and her precious little boy was the cutest. He had soft curls, chubby cheeks, and pretty light brown eyes.

My brother was sitting there looking every bit the proud papa. There was something that didn't sit right with me though. His little girl Princess looked just like him; nose, eyes, and ears. She was precious and as precious as her son was, he couldn't be my brother's baby. I didn't know how he couldn't see that wasn't his child. I guess because he was just too happy to finally have a son. But maybe I was wrong about that. For all their sakes, I hoped I was wrong.

I was in the process of planning me and Zay's wedding, which was six months from now. I was so excited. I knew it might seem cliché, but I wanted us to be married on Valentine's Day. We were so in love and I wanted the world to feel our love on that day. I had hired a wedding planner named Maggie and she was wonderful. I didn't know how I would've gotten this far without Maggie.

We decided we didn't want the traditional church wedding, so instead we were using a private club with the most beautiful scenery. I wanted calla lilies in my bouquet with white roses tied together with a beautiful red ribbon with crystals on it. I also had made plans with my bridesmaids to go to

Kleinfeld's to find my wedding dress. My mom was so excited to be a part of this wedding and she couldn't wait to go shopping for the dresses.

"Are you gonna let Malaysia be a part of the wedding?" My mom asked one day while we were looking through bridal magazines.

"I was thinking about it. But I'm not sure mom," I said.

"I think you should ask her because she doesn't have anyone. With her mom gone, she doesn't have any other family members. I just feel so bad for her because she just had a baby and her mom isn't here to help her."

"At least Princeton has been there for her since she had the baby. That girl, Zoey don't want him to take Princess anywhere near Malaysia. I think she's just jealous that he's with Malaysia and not her, but she's wrong for doing that because he's a good dad," I said. "When you think about it, who is she hurting? Just Princess because that little girl loves her daddy."

Don't think for a second that I forgot about my brother betraying our family and killing my dad. I wanted to kill his ass a long time ago, but Zay wouldn't let me do anything while I was pregnant. Now that my baby was here, and I was given the okay by the doctor to have sex, that meant I was okay to pull the trigger.

I had asked my mom to take Za'Nya home with her for the next couple of days. She readily accepted because she couldn't wait to spend time with my baby girl. I also knew that Lacey was looking forward to playing auntie to her niece.

Zay didn't know it yet, but I was ready to get in my brother's ass. I knew I should just let it go because this could destroy our family, but I couldn't help how I felt. I needed him gone, so he couldn't hurt anyone else anymore. I had got with Chico and Chance behind Zay's back and I knew he was going to be pissed. He kept saying I wasn't about that life, but I was about to show him a whole different side of Lexus.

I couldn't share my plans with anyone because I didn't want anyone to try and dissuade me from doing what was necessary for me to move on. Zay was at the office, so once my mom left with Za'Nya, I grabbed my phone and hit the call button. As much as I would miss my baby girl since we had never been apart overnight before, this was something I had to do for my own peace of mind.

"Waddup," Chance answered.

"Can you talk?" I asked.

I could hear him say, "Aye y'all, I need to take this call. I'll be back in a minute."

I heard scuffling and then a door close before he came back on the phone.

"Yea, waddup."

"Hey, what's up with the Princeton situation?" I asked.

"Man, we been trying to snatch that nigga, but he's always with either the baby or Malaysia and the baby. I can't nab that nigga when he's with the kid because I don't want nothing to happen to your nephew," he said.

"Yea, I don't want anything to happen to my nephew either."

"That's what I'm saying. I just don't know how else we can get that nigga, yo," he said.

"Does Zay know anything about this?"

"Nah, I ain't no snitch. Zay, my boss and all, but you the original boss man's baby girl. I feel that I owe it to you and to him to avenge his death, even if it's his own son. It's just something I have to do," he said. "But aye, are you sure you wanna do this? I mean, he is your only brother."

"He stopped being my brother the moment I found out that he was responsible for my dad's death. I can't seem to forgive him for that, ya know?"

"Yea, I know. I would feel the same way if someone had taken out my ol' man. I just don't know if I'd be able to pull the trigger on my own brother. But aye, to each his own. When I get the chance to get that nigga, I'll let you know," Chance said.

"Thanks Chance."

"No problem, ma," he said.

"Okay well, Za'Nya is with my mom for the next couple of days, so if you can make something happen during that time, I'd be grateful. I just need to get his ass," I said.

"Understood and I'll hit you up if something changes."

"Cool. Oh, and remember that Zay doesn't know anything, so please don't let anything slip out," I said.

"C'mon now, you know me better than that."

"Alright," I said and ended the call.

I was itching for my brother to make a move without Malaysia or the baby. It was almost as if he knew that his life was in danger and he was hiding behind the baby. I just needed to get this shit over with because I felt as if I was losing my mind waiting on something to happen. A few minutes later, my phone rang, so I picked up and checked to see who was calling.

"Hey baby," I cooed into the phone.

"Hey, what you up to?" Zay asked.

"Nothing much. I was actually thinking about going do some dress hunting for the wedding since my mom has Za'Nya."

"Your mom has Za'Nya? For how long?" he asked.

"A couple of nights," I said.

"Really? What brought that on?"

"What you mean?"

"I mean, do you have appointments or shit to do that you couldn't do it with the baby?" he asked.

"Yea, I actually do have a few things planned."

"Do some of those things include me?"

"Everything I do is for you," I said.

"Good because guess who will be home soon. I miss you baby and I miss making love to you," he said.

"I miss you too, baby."

"Gimme a couple of hours and I'm coming home to tear dat ass up," he said as we broke into laughter.

"Boy, you so crazy," I laughed.

"You bout to see just how crazy I am," he said.

"Well, bring it on because I miss my man," I said.

"Bet," he said and ended the call.

Well, I hoped nothing jumped off with Zay coming home early and all. I knew he was anxious to get his freak on and so was I. With me being on restrictions for six weeks and then the baby waking up all times of the day, it was hard to have some privacy and get busy when we were both so tired.

Zay had been really busy with work, so he always came home tired. I missed my man between my legs, eating my pussy and stroking me with his big dick. Now that I knew he was coming home early, I was gonna make this the best night ever.

I planned to cook and light some candles, with soft music and sexy lingerie. I was gonna make my man really happy tonight. I went upstairs and ran a bubble bath, so I could be clean and fresh whenever he came in. I used the lavender and vanilla scent because it always calmed my nerves. And with the way I was feeling about my brother, my nerves needed all the calming they could get. I slipped in the tub and let the scent take over my brain.

It felt so soothing that I must have fallen asleep because next thing I knew, Zay was tapping my shoulder. I jumped up because he startled me.

"Hey babe," he said with a smile.

"Hey, when did you get here?" I asked.

"A few minutes ago. I called for you, but you didn't answer, so I came looking for you since your car was in the garage. I didn't expect to find you in here though," he said with a chuckle.

"I must have fallen asleep. What time is it?" I asked as I stood to get out the tub.

"Like six in the evening," he said, helping me out.

He grabbed a towel and dried me off.

"Ummm, you smell so good. Can I taste you?" he asked.

"You know you don't even have to ask," I said with a smile.

He didn't even wait for me to make it to the bed. He just got on his knees and began licking between my thighs. I came instantly because it had been a long time since my man had touched me there, let alone feasted there. Oh God, my knees were so weak, I almost fell to the floor.

"Babe, can we move this into the bedroom. My legs can't take it anymore," I said, looking into his beautiful eyes.

"Yea, but don't think you getting away from me," he said.

"Never." I said as I twisted my ass and he followed me, almost as if he was hypnotized or something.

I laid back in the bed and opened my legs to receive either his big dick or his tongue. At this point, it didn't matter to me which one he used; I was ready. He stuck his face between my legs again and began to lick and suck me until I had another orgasm. I smiled as I watched him lick up all my sweet juices. He slurped the juice from my pussy like it was a popsicle. I held his head as I fucked his tongue; he loved it when I did that.

He ran his tongue along my asshole and that drove me crazy. He sucked on my clit until my legs shivered. He lifted his face up and wiped my juices from his mouth. He smiled at me as he kneeled in the bed and I sat up and kissed him hungrily. He took off his shirt, revealing his sexy abs and chest. Oh God, he was fine!

He stood up and removed his pants and boxers, revealing his magic stick. I called it the magic stick because when he fucked me with it, I felt like I was being sent somewhere far away. He moved closer to me and I took his stick in my hands, stroking it as I watched him. His eyes were filled with love and lust and that made me even hornier than I was before.

I finally took my tongue and licked around the big mushroom head while stroking his dick up and down. I wrapped my lips around it and inch by inch, it disappeared down my throat. Until I got with Zay, I didn't even know how to deep throat a dick. Zay had taught me so much over the past two years and I cherished every moment and lesson. I sucked and stroked until his knees got as weak as mine were a few minutes ago.

"Babe, let me get some of that good cookie," he said.

I wasted no time getting on my back and opening my legs wide, allowing him full access to my treasured goodies. He climbed on top of me and stuffed me with his magic stick. Oh God! I hadn't had it in three and a half months, so it felt good. I rotated my hips, grinding my pelvis into his, but receiving his dick. I couldn't take it all in at once, especially since my pussy was so tight.

I brought his face to mine and stuck my tongue in his mouth. I kissed him like my life depended on it. He was a great kisser. He was the ultimate lover. He was a fabulous father. I really felt as though I had the perfect man. Well, no man was perfect, but he was definitely the perfect man for me.

He continued to work me out until I had all of him inside me. I had missed that feeling so much and was glad that our baby wasn't here because she definitely wouldn't have gotten any sleep tonight.

"Let me get that good thang from the back," he said.

I turned over and he got behind me, spanking my ass with that big dick. I turned to look at him, biting down on my lip because I knew how much he liked seeing me do that.

"C'mon babe, put it in and stop teasing me." I said as I looked at him and winked.

"You want this?" he asked, smacking my ass with it.

"Yaaasssssss!" I said.

"You sure?" He asked as he rubbed it on the opening to my hole.

"Yaaaasssss! Oh God, please just put it in!" I cried.

He shoved his dick inside me, and I moaned so loud it sounded like a scream. He smacked my ass as he plowed deeper and deeper into me.

"This what you wanted?" he asked in a husky voice.

"Oh yes! Fuck me, baby!" I begged.

He drove it in deeper and deeper, harder and harder until I was delirious. I missed this so much. I missed my man. I missed his lovemaking. I missed all that. And I could tell he missed me too when he released that heavy load he had been carrying all this time. I could barely move as I collapsed on the bed. He laid down next to me and took me in his arms, holding me close.

"I love you so much," I said.

"I love you to the moon and back, baby," he said.

Soon after I heard him snoring softly, so I shut my eyes and joined him in slumber.

CHAPTER EIGHTEEN

Malaysia

Since I had given birth to Prince, things between Princeton and I had been wonderful. It was almost like he was a whole new man. He had been so attentive ever since we came home with the baby. He cooked, cleaned, fed the baby, and changed him. He did everything a good dad would do to help the mom care for their child. When he said he was a good dad, he really meant that. He was wonderful with our son and he was even better with me.

My baby was the most precious and beautiful child I had ever laid eyes on. He had smooth curly hair and chubby little cheeks. In the back of my mind, I knew I was playing with fire. I knew my son was Anthony's child the minute they handed him to me. I mean, he was the spitting image of his daddy, his real daddy. But Princeton was so happy to have a son, I didn't think he even noticed my son's uncanny resemblance to Anthony.

He was just the best father and I didn't know how to break that news to him. How do you tell a man that the child he thought was his from day one wasn't his? He woke up in the middle of the night to give Prince his bottles and change his diapers. I had to have a cesarean section because my baby's head was too big to pass him naturally. I had pushed for three long hours before my doctor finally decided to cut me and take him out. I was exhausted because I had been in labor for ten hours. Even though I had a hard labor, I wouldn't have changed a thing. I loved being a mother and the labor was worth it.

"Hey baby," Princeton said, giving me a kiss.

"Hey you," I said, smiling.

"What are your plans for today?"

"I thought I would go visit my mom's grave. I haven't been to see her since the funeral, and I miss her. I need to go visit her. I need to tell her how precious her grandson is and how good you have been to us. I want to give her a reason to smile down on us," I said.

"That's sweet! You know I love you, right?"

"Yea, I know now."

"You really have had my back, ya know? Do you remember when I told Zoey that we were engaged?" he asked.

"Yea, but you were just lying to grind her gears. You know that baby mama of yours is crazy and has a few screws loose. I don't know why you told her that."

"Well, I told her that because that was something that I planned for us at some point during our relationship. Look babe, I didn't mean to fall in love with you, but I did. To be honest, I didn't think that I could love another woman after Alize cheated on me. But you changed my mind about love. You changed me and thanks to you, I'm a better person," he said.

"Babe, thank you for the kind words. I love you too, but where is this going? I mean, why are you talking about Alize?" I asked.

I knew he killed her, but as much as I loved him, hearing her name roll off his tongue so easily made me cringe a little. It was kind of sad that we couldn't pick the ones we fell in love with. I mean, our hearts rocked to the beat of its own drum set, ya know?

"I am saying this because I think, no, scratch that. I feel that we belong together. I love you, Malaysia. I love the life that we're building for our son and everything about you. You gave me my first baby boy and I love you so much for that. You put up with so much of my bullshit and proved to be a true ride or die chick. I swear, I didn't think I could love again, but baby, I love you. It would make me so happy if you would marry me," he said.

The fuck did he say? He wanted to marry me? Surely, I was being punked right now and any moment, people would jump out the bedrooms and closets telling me what a fool I was. But instead of that happening, Princeton dug in his pocket and pulled out a little blue box from Tiffany's.

My heart began to beat so loud that I knew he had to be hearing it too. He opened the box and in it was a huge diamond engagement ring. I mean, the ring had to be at least five carats and it was set in platinum, at least that was what I thought. I opened my mouth to say something, but no words would come out. I was absolutely speechless and that didn't happen to me very often.

"Can you say something please? I mean, do you want me to get on one knee? Will that make it easier for you to say yes?" he asked flashing that handsome smile.

He got down on one knee and put the ring in front of me. "Malaysia Denise Hughes, will you marry me?"

What was I supposed to say? I mean, how could I marry him knowing that he killed Alize and Roz? How could I marry him knowing that he ordered a hit on his own father? How could I marry him knowing that the son he thought was his was actually Anthony's? How could I marry him when I still carried around all these feelings for Zay? Oh my God! My mind was reeling because the questions just kept coming. I shouldn't marry him. We couldn't be together.

I knew all the reasons why we shouldn't get married. But instead of saying no, I just smiled, stuck out my left hand, and said, "Yes."

He pulled the ring out of the beautiful box and slipped it on my finger. My hand was shaking profusely as I received the beautiful ring. He pulled me close and kissed me deeply.

"I can't believe we're engaged!" I said.

"Yea, well the proof is on your finger," he said as he beamed happily.

"Well, as much as I'd like to stay with you, babe, I really want to go see my mom. Can you watch Prince while I'm gone please?"

"You don't have to say please, babe; he's my son too. I'd be more than happy to watch our son, but how long will you be, babe? I have to run by the warehouse," he said.

"Okay, I'll try not to be too long," I said.

He kissed me on the lips and released me. I kissed my baby boy and left the apartment. The police still had no idea who killed my mom and that was definitely starting to anger me. How could they not have any leads after almost four months? My mom was one of the sweetest women in our area. It pained me knowing that she would help anyone that needed it, but no one would come forward to help catch her killer.

I got in my new BMW that Princeton purchased for me a few days ago and headed to the gravesite to see my mom. I needed her to know that I was okay, and that Princeton and I were in a great place, so she could rest easy. I just needed her to know that she didn't have to worry about me because he was taking care of me. I needed her to know that he wasn't the monster she thought he was. He really was a good man, despite what acts he had committed before today.

He said I made him a better man, so I could thank God for one thing.

CHAPTER NINETEEN

Princeton

I was now an engaged man. Who would have thought that Malaysia would've given me a son? Who would have thought that I'd fall in love with my little sister's best friend? Who would've thought that one day I'd be engaged to Malaysia? If someone had told me two years ago that me and Malaysia would have a baby and be engaged, I would've told them they were a damn liar. But I really did care about Malaysia. I mean, I loved her, and I wanted her to be my wife, so we could raise our son together as a family.

My son began to cry, so I grabbed a bottle and fixed him one. He was a big eater; like father, like son I guess. I picked up my little bug-a-boo and fed him his bottle. When he was done with the bottle, I burped him, changed his diaper and rocked him back to sleep.

I put him in his crib and pulled out my laptop to check my bank account. I had a friend on the inside that was cleaning up my money for me, so every so often I made a deposit. I didn't need it to be a huge deposit, but I liked using a debit card, so I needed money in an account for that.

My phone rang, and I checked the caller ID. I didn't recognize the number, but I answered anyway.

"Mr. Clark?" asked the voice on the other end.

"Who wants to know?" I asked.

"Mr. Clark, this is Detective Ashford. I need you to come to the police station today because I have some questions for you," the detective said.

"I'm sorry detective, but now isn't a good time. My fiancée isn't here right now and I'm taking care of my newborn son. What's this about?" I asked.

"I think you know what this is about, Mr. Clark. What time would be a good time for you to come in?" he asked.

"I don't know. I guess I could come in when my fiancée gets back."

"See to it that you come in today, Mr. Clark or we'll have to come and escort you down to the station," he said.

"That ain't necessary, man. I'll be there as soon as my fiancée makes it back home," I said as I ended the call. "Fuck! What the hell could this man have to talk to me about now?"

I was getting ready to go lie down for a nap with my son when my phone rang again. I picked up when I saw that it was August calling me. August was one of my top lieutenants since Zay got fired. I didn't think I'd be able to replace Zay because he was a great soldier. I met August not long after we put the hit on those Nigerians. As a matter of fact, he was a Nigerian who relocated here to find work.

He had proved himself to be quite the hitman and he had proven his loyalty. I didn't know why I couldn't get over the fact that Zay was with my sister. I had tried over the past year to accept it, but I just couldn't. I mean, he had gone left when I told him to go right. A nigga like that just couldn't be trusted.

"Waddup August?" I answered.

"Hey, we need you to come down to the warehouse, man," he said.

"Wassup, yo. I mean, I have my son because Malaysia went to run an errand. Can it wait a little while?"

"Nah, some shit just went down, and we need you here ASAP!" he said.

"What's the fuckin' deal? Like, what's so important that you can't handle it?"

"Them Nigerians is here man and they mad as fuck!" he said.

"Fuck! What the fuck do they want?"

"They want you," he said.

"I'm on my way!" I said as I ended the call. "Dammit! What the fuck do those Nigerians want? FUCK! FUCK! FUCK!" I yelled.

I knew setting them mofos up was gonna come back to haunt me. I only did it because Zay had stolen my dad's connect. How could he turn around and do business with those Nigerians when I had my dad killed for that same fucking reason? The shit was absolutely ridiculous! Who the fuck told them that we set them up? How the fuck did they find that out?

I picked up my phone and hit the talk button.

"Hey baby," Malaysia answered.

"Hey babe, are you still at the graveyard?" I asked.

"Yea, I actually just got here because of the traffic. Is everything okay?" she asked.

"Yea, everything is fine."

"Are you sure? You sound a little nervous."

"I'm positive. Finish your visit and I'll see you when you get here," I said.

"Okay baby. I love you," she said.

"I love you too. I really mean that girl." I said with a smile that I knew she could hear in my voice.

I hung up with Malaysia feeling better than ever about our relationship. Who would have thought that I could be happy with her? I didn't expect to fall for Malaysia, but I did.

I had no plans to go anywhere, but then I got a call from August about the Nigerians being at the warehouse, so I had no choice. I didn't mean for any of this shit to come back to bite me in the ass, but it did. But why now? Why now when everything was so perfect between me and Malaysia? How could things have gone from good to bad so fast?

I went upstairs to get my son dressed and put him in his car seat. I grabbed my keys, headed out the door, strapped my son in the back seat, and jumped in my Mercedes. I didn't live but 20 minutes from the warehouse, so it wouldn't take me long to get there. I was almost at the warehouse when I noticed a black truck with huge tires following me. I wanted to make sure it was really following me, so I veered right onto a back road and the truck did the same. I sped up and it did the same. I didn't want to go too fast since I had my son in the car, but I couldn't take a chance of the same thing that happened to Malaysia happening to me.

It was times like these that I wished my dad didn't have his warehouse so far away from the hustle and bustle of the city. Where his office was located, there was nothing around it but green fields and back roads with little to no traffic.

I picked up speed and the big truck picked up speed too. In a matter of minutes, all hell broke loose. One minute, I was racing to get away from the driver of the truck and the next minute, I was ducking and dodging bullets that were being fired at me.

The truck was now beside me and bullets were flying into my car from the automatic weapon they were using. I felt myself get hit once, then twice as I tried to maintain control of the luxury vehicle. Was this really the end of the road for me? I knew I had done a lot of shit in an effort to maintain the powerful boss that I was when I took over my dad's business, but I didn't deserve to go out like this.

I could hear Prince screaming from his car seat in the back and I prayed that he'd make it through this alive. I must've been hit several times because I felt myself wanting to pass out and needing to close my eyes. I tried my best to steer my vehicle since I was almost at the warehouse, but I was hit too many times and felt myself careening off the main road.

I hit the brakes and the car came to a stop in the green field. Right before I passed out, the last thing I noticed was that Prince wasn't crying anymore. God please save my son. Take me but save my baby boy.

Malaysia

I was on my way back home from the cemetery, feeling really good after having a heart to heart talk with my mom. I was smiling from the ear to ear when the shrill sound of my ringing phone brought me out of my daydream. I looked at the caller ID but didn't recognize the number. I decided to answer anyway because you never know who could be calling with some news.

"Hello."

"Malaysia! Malaysia, Princeton's been in an accident!" August screamed into the phone.

"What! Oh my God! WHERE IS HE AND WHERE IS MY BABY?" I screamed back.

"The baby was in the car with him and Malaysia, it doesn't look good!"

"WHERE ARE THEY?!!" I asked as I broke into tears.

"They were airlifted to Brookdale University. Hurry!" he said.

I hung up with August and called Ms. Yvonne. I just didn't want to believe what that man said was true. She answered on the first ring.

"Malaysia, where are you?" she asked breathlessly.

"Ms. Yvonne, I just got a phone call about Princeton and the baby," I said.

"Yes, I know. I'm on my way to the hospital now."

"So, it's true? This isn't some sick joke and my baby might be dead?" I asked.

"I'm sorry sweetheart, but it isn't a joke. You need to get to the hospital as soon as possible and I'll meet you there," she said.

"Okay," I said and hung up.

I pulled over to the side of the road and began to cry harder than I've ever cried before. How could God be so cruel? First, my mom and now my baby boy. The last time I cried this hard was when my mom was killed. And now, my baby was probably dead, along with the man I loved and was planning to marry. How the hell could this have happened? Where was Princeton when this happened? He was supposed to be at home with the baby.

Oh my God! Just a couple of hours ago, everything was fine. Now, my baby and my man had been shot and they might be dead. Oh God, please let them be alright. The last thing I needed was to lose them. "Please God, if you're listening,

please let them be alright," I prayed as I careened
back onto the highway and headed to the hospital.

To be continued...

Made in the USA
Monee, IL
17 June 2022

98213677R00166